Engaging Passion

Ela Bell

DEDICATION

To my husband for his continued support.

CONTENTS

ACKNOWLEDGMENTS

Thank you to my husband, whose editing and insights helped make the book a reality. Thanks to W. Stevens for her sharp read of the text. Kudos to Tatiana Villa for super book covers; you rock! Thanks to my local friends, who are encouraging and positive. Finally, thanks to technology, without which the book would not have been written. Thanks to Mom who read to us before we could talk.

1 FAMILY AND FEAR

Beth looked up from her laptop computer and noticed movement. The house was normally quiet. Only she and a bare bones staff remained as part of the McKeans' household. As an agent, she always kept a revolver nearby and she reached to the back of her chair where the gun rested in its holster. The snap on the top made a clicking noise. Too loud, she thought. Anyone listening would know she was ready. A bullet buzzed by her head and stuck in the corkboard on the wall behind her. She took a deep breath. She had trained for these moments but had had very few in the years she had worked for the McKeans — partly because they were so good at protecting their daughter and their whereabouts. But they were gone — perhaps dead — and their daughter, Val, had married the love of her life. This attack could mean that they were indeed dead or in deep hiding. Why else would someone be here — three years after their disappearance?

She ducked under the kitchen island counter and pulled the weapon close to her. She noticed a figure in black

1

creeping toward her in the reflection of the glass door leading to the patio. She waited, holding her breath. As the black-clad legs came closer, she stood quickly, took aim and fired. It was over in a moment.

She walked over to the body and pulled the black ski mask from his head. His looks suggested the group that the McKeans were after when they disappeared from their daughter's life. Yes, that group might have employed this character. She checked for a pulse and was certain he was dead. Then, she checked the other rooms in the house to be certain the man did not bring company. Assured that he had come alone, she called Ramon Jose on her cell. Val thought Ramon was a middle-aged man, who simply worked in the garden, but his actual job was guarding and he was much younger than Val suspected. But to women the age of Val, men who were made to look as old as Ramon seemed ancient. Ramon came in through the back door, took one look at the blood pooling around the figure lying on the floor and vaulted into action. He dragged the man's body out of the way and then called for disposal assistance.

"You all right?" he asked Beth. He felt an unreasonable amount of protectiveness for Beth. She avoided him but knew that he was smitten with her.

"Sure," she said. "Just a little surprised. I suppose this one won't be revealing any secrets. What do you suppose he was after?"

"Maybe he thought Val would be here," Ramon said.

"If he did, they have some severely outdated information."

"Mmm. That's not surprising. That can happen in the underworld. Information can get twisted." As they stood there talking, two agents walked in, zipped the dead man in a bag and carried him to a waiting van. They drove away without much conversation. Beth informed the agents about what happened, and they had her sign a form.

Attempts like this had happened before, but never so bold, never so direct. Most of the others were break-ins or attempted break-ins and always incidents that were far apart — at least six months between events. Whoever was doing this must be getting desperate.

Most of the mess of the forced entries revealed the perpetrators were looking for something near the computer equipment. However, nothing seemed to be stolen, just moved and searched. Everything was so neat that it looked like an inside job. She wondered whether the criminals were looking for something the McKeans had on one of the hidden travel drives. The cleanup crew was away before she could consider her next move. She stood there, staring into the large backyard; it was a typical cloudy autumn day in rural west Connecticut

"Hey," Ramon said, snapping his fingers in front of her face. "Come on, Beth." He moved closer to her and put his muscled arms around her. He hugged her to him. He could feel her shudder. They might have been a couple if she would only give him a chance. She was forever declaring that he was too young for her. He was assigned to guard the McKean girl but also felt it necessary to protect Beth. He could see lots of potential in a long-term relationship with her, but over the years she had held him firmly at a distance. Since he didn't believe in mixing business with pleasure, he had kept his distance, patient to wait until the time was right.

"It doesn't get easier does it, Ramon?" she said, sighing. She stood back and took a good look at him. His broad shoulders and muscled arms had been the source of many of her fantasies. His trim waist led down to muscled thighs, apparent through his jeans. His dark skin shone with the health of youth but also with the health of good habits. His black hair, dark eyes and Roman nose gave him a classic beauty. Beth shivered with awareness but fought to control herself.

3

"No, it never does," he said, smiling. He knew she was perusing him sexually but was trying hard not to acknowledge it. "But it was either him or you. You know that."

"Yes, I know, but it still feels . . .." He took a step toward her to wrap her in his arms.

He lifted her chin and looked into her eyes. "Now is not the time to crumble," he said with a crisp Latin accent. "You have plans, right?"

"Yes, my sister."

"Then put this behind you. I'll deal with it. I'm going to stay with the house a bit longer than I planned. I'll be certain you aren't being targeted or followed. Later, I'll close everything up and let Val know that we've put the house up for sale."

"Are you sure that's what she wants?" she asked.

"Her parents are gone, Beth. There is no reason to keep the house or for us to remain. There are better things we can do with our time."

Beth took a deep breath. "You're right." Ramon and Beth got to work cleaning up the bloodstains before the mess could set on the kitchen tile.

Ethel Elizabeth Larsen had been one of those quiet, intelligent young women who graduated first in her class and faded away into what her peers thought was obscurity. She'd taken a civil service exam; then she was recruited by special service agencies. There was nothing exceptional about her, she thought. Many of her peers disagreed and thought she and her twin, Gina, were outstanding beauties. However, her brown hair, brown eyes and olive skin helped her blend in most anywhere. She had a talent for languages and oddly for higher math as well. Her recruiters were stunned by her unassuming intelligence. Her twin sister was equally intelligent but opted to avoid public service for a "normal" life as a suburban wife in the West. Beth was eager to return home to her family, what little she had left, her sister, aunt and uncle, and to the subtropical island she called home, Galveston, Texas.

However, Beth, as her sister and friends called her, was not interested in staying on the little island where they grew up. Too many bad memories lingered; her parents' death, when she was young, was one of them. Then, there were her failures as a woman — all of that happened in Galveston. But she was finished with public service now. The protection service for which she worked had assigned her to guard the lives of a family that worked for the agency. She'd often felt unfulfilled and underutilized in the service. She was to work undercover assisting the husband and wife as part of their team and to "be there" for any contingencies. Over the years, and there were many, it seemed there was no end to the number of peccadillos the couple encountered as part of their work. She had worked with them on and off in various roles for about 20 years and had become friends with Helen and her daughter, Val.

When officials in the service learned of her abilities with computers and research, they put her to work, not only for the McKeans, but also for other agents. It didn't matter where she was physically; just that she had access to some of the most sensitive files using the most up-to-date and powerful servers and computers. She could hack into anything and could find any kind of information. If she couldn't find it, she knew who could. She had developed a network of cyber friends over the years. They trusted her, and she in turn trusted them. Together, they worked on problems that defied the agents who worked in headquarters.

In her last term of service as the McKeans' housekeeper, she didn't do any real housework. That was for the maids and cook, whom she hired. However, her secret room in the house led to a cache of computers and servers. The gear helped her to do most any job from the McKeans' home. But this wasn't really home anymore. The

McKeans were so wealthy, they could afford to keep her here indefinitely, and she'd been paid well — both by the agency and the McKeans. A draft continued to appear mysteriously in her bank account each month. She considered that since the house really belonged to the McKeans, it wasn't ever really *her* home. It had taken her a while to realize it was time to move on. Even the McKeans' daughter, Val, had given up. Val had searched for her parents for a while but given up most of her inquires after she married.

Val McKean had become like a daughter to Beth, but she was all grown up now. Beth recalled the many moments when she was able to indulge her love of cooking to please Val after her parents were gone. She had given her life to three people who no longer needed her. In the lonely days that followed the disappearance of the couple, Beth realized that she wanted what they had, but it was likely too late. She was past the age when women typically started families. Still, she'd been doing this for too long; she was weary and wanted a different kind of life. She'd put in her retirement papers long ago, and approval had finally come. Now, she had a new life to make. It was scary. What could possibly be in the world for her now?

She took some of her most treasured items, a powerful personal computer that she'd bought herself. She'd copied sensitive files and important information onto travel drives that she kept carefully hidden and proceeded to secure everything else. She took the documents left behind by Val, those that identified Val's parents as having worked under a number of aliases. She and Ramon shared an additional goodbye, which she tried to make as impersonal as possible; after all, this was work, professional work.

Men sometimes assumed a woman couldn't separate her professional and personal lives, but that was something she prided herself on. They shook hands impersonally at first; however, Ramon wasn't going to stand for it. He pulled her into his arms and gave her a tight hug; she finished gathering her things and locked the front door, knowing that Ramon had his own set of keys. As she looked back at the house one last time, she knew that Ramon was watching her from somewhere on the property. She got into her Honda CRV and drove west, headed for Texas.

During the long drive, she contemplated a plan for discovering what had happened to Val's parents, the McKeans. If she could reach a friend of hers, Zah, who knew much about the underworld through digital and Internet research, she might get a lead. Zah, however, had been out of touch for quite some time and any communication lately with the cyber whiz kid was fleeting and vague. She would need to tap into other sources before she knew where to look. She ran that plan through her head time and again as she took Interstate 95 and then 65. The drive should have taken a day, but she stopped along the way in D.C. and Atlanta to see the sites. In addition, Beth had mapped her way around as many long bridges as she could. Crossing water bothered her.

It was a true source of wonder for her remaining family members that she'd held on to such an unreasonable fear of large bodies of water. After all, the people of Galveston lived on a 27 mile-long island — they were surrounded by water, a beautiful bay on the north side and the Gulf of Mexico to the south. Her sister lived not far from where their parents had died in a boating accident when they were children. The water didn't bother Gina at all. But, looking out at large bodies of water always reminded Beth that their parents had died tragically and unnecessarily on the bay. Beth thought that if she could return to the area and to the bay in particular, she might someday overcome her fear. She promised herself to work on it; she had to master it some day. When she arrived in

Galveston, tired from a couple days of driving, and wanting only to sleep, she hugged her sister tightly, tearing up a bit as they both looked into identical faces and laughed.

"What took you so long?" Gina asked.

"Work, Gina," Beth said, holding her sister at arm's length. "You know what it means to have to work. Wait, no you don't." They teased each other whenever they talked about the comparatively soft life Gina had led. The two had a special relationship – shared dreams sometimes.

When their joyful greetings and small talk subsided, Beth unloaded the sensitive computer equipment she had brought with her. She had had the wisdom to stay overnight in a hotel before driving the remaining distance to Galveston, so she wasn't so exhausted that she couldn't visit with her sister and do those things that needed doing before she settled in. The two-story, light-blue house with some cedar siding for the roof and spacious interiors decorated in light blue and yellow was on Sportsman's Road.

She and Gina communicated regularly, but Beth hadn't seen her sister's new home. Gina's husband, an executive at a tech company, had made his fortune and built the house for his wife as an incentive to marry. They had lived in Houston for most of his career, but Gina preferred the house in Galveston, with its peaceful vistas and plentiful opportunities for birding.

When Gina finally agreed to marry Jim, he was overjoyed. They had had many happy years together before he died in a car accident, leaving Gina well provided for. Gina never remarried. They had one child, who was now an adult and living in China. So Gina had the large house to herself. Next door, she had a small guest cottage that she lent to their aunt and uncle, Madeline and Gerald. The elderly couple visited from time to time, but usually kept company with their friends or with one another.

Both were reasonably healthy, in their mid-70s and

constantly involved in one hare-brained scheme after another. Gerald loved to fish off the pier in the bay, and Maddy, as the family called her, loved to play cards with the neighboring women and with Gina, from time to time. Gina and Beth unpacked Beth's CRV and stored her things in a wing of Gina's home. The wing had soft beige carpeting and light blue curtains and bed clothing. Gina showed her sister around the home, making a special trip up to the cupola to show Beth the vast gulf and bay scenery. Ibis stalked prey in the marshlands, a kite perched on a nearby telephone pole, egrets waded through the brackish water, and mottled ducks and cormorants hunted for meals. A flock of pelicans flew over the bay to the north. Gina helped Beth spot them in her scope, and a sense of peace came over Beth as she realized she really was home. "It's peaceful up here," Gina said, breathing deeply.

"Do you miss him?"

"Jim?" Gina asked, a soft look on her face as she stared out at the bay.

"Of course, but being here makes me feel near him," Gina said.

"I don't know how you do it," Beth said. "Not only do you have the memories of your husband here … but what about our parents?" Beth looked out into the distance over the bay. It was just over there, in that direction … that was the area they thought their parents had drowned.

"Actually, I feel closer to all of them here," Gina said. "You need to look at it in a particular way to not let that bother you. What about you? Have you ever gotten over your fear of water because of Mom and Pop?"

Beth took a deep breath. The wind blew her hair into her face and she smoothed it out of the way. "I don't think I'll ever get over that fear. I used to dream of their death, of drowning with them. I'd wake up covered in sweat and realize that it was Mom talking to me."

"Hmmm. What did she say?" Gina smiled at her sister,

inviting her to open up. Beth allowed several seconds to pass before she responded. She knew her sister was not teasing her as they often felt some of the same emotions. Sometimes, Gina dreamed of something that might happen to Beth or Beth dreamed of something that might happen to Gina. They were connected in ways that twins sometimes are.

"Nothing really," Beth said. "I think she was just wanting me to come up for air. To live."

"Yes," Gina said. "So did you get over your fear of water? I know that you wouldn't be here unless you'd worked on it over the years."

"You're right. I did. I saw a doctor about it, a shrink, for some time. The therapists worked with me. It's not like I can't swim. Mom and Pop made sure we had good lessons from the time we were very young. But. …"

"But it's harder to get in the water since their death," Gina said.

"It's not just getting in the water; it's going over bodies of water. Or getting in a boat."

"How did you hide this from the service for so many years?"

"I didn't. I passed all my tests and physicals and simply went on with my work. I didn't share the fear until much later. By then, it was clear I would be stationed where there was no threat from large bodies of water. I stayed mostly in the states, inland, so no problem."

"I guess you got over it to some extent or you wouldn't be here. My house is practically surrounded by water," Gina said. "Will you cope with that?"

"Sure," Beth grinned, then gulped. "No problem." They both laughed.

They settled in for a visit in Gina's sitting room, near the open kitchen.

"Are you hungry, thirsty?" Gina asked. "I know you

could eat something, Beth; you never turn down food. Do you still enjoy cooking?"

"That was one of the joys of living north in such an isolated area," Beth said. "Plenty of time to cook." Beth grinned, agreeing that she could use a little nourishment. Dressed in a flowing burnt orange tunic and loose white pants, her soft leather sandals making a soft swishing sound on the tile, Gina prepared a late lunch.

"So have you heard from Tim?" Beth asked, thinking of Gina's son.

"He's doing fine. I heard from him just last week. He's enjoying China but thinks he'll move on to Japan for a while."

"I guess he inherited the family talent for languages," Beth said.

"He works at it, Beth, just like rest of us. You know that," her sister smiled. She put a salad out for the two of them, and they dug in.

"Do you still enjoy cooking, Beth?" Beth nodded, continuing to carve up the salad.

"So what are your plans, Beth?"

"I think I want to get the lay of the land first to see whether there are any possibilities out there."

"You want to work again part-time … I mean for the service?"

"No, that's not what I want. I'm finished with that. But I do have some problems I'm trying to work out." She paused, wondering whether she could trust her sister, her fork hanging in the air as she considered. Gina knew that look. The two had always had a special bond. One could never experience something urgent without the other knowing about it. Gina reached over and squeezed her sister's hand, giving her that look that meant, "Hey, this is me, your sister."

"I can trust you to keep this quiet?"

"If this is something sensitive, let's don't talk about it

now." Beth shrugged her shoulders and agreed, looking around. She mouthed the word "big ears," and her sister shrugged her shoulders too, nodding her head.

"Well, it's about time you brought yourself home, young lady," a familiar voice said as she entered the sliding glass door from the deck. Maddy walked slowly with a cane but managed to defy her years. Her gray hair shone and her brown eyes twinkled as she smiled at her niece. She made her way over to Beth, who stood up and walked into her aunt's arms. The cane dropped to the floor. Maddy and Gerald were the only parental figures the girls had had in those teenage years after their parents had died in the boating accident. They moved to a seating area near the kitchen. Gina began to clear away the dishes and load them in the dishwasher. Beth picked up her aunt's wooden cane, full of gnarls, and led her to a firm chair.

"So, you're finally back," Maddy said with a deep sigh. "We thought you'd forgotten where you live, Beth. It's not as if you need to work, you know."

"I did, Aunt Maddy; you know that. I needed to make a life for myself." Aunt Maddy and Uncle Gerald had retired comfortably, he from the oil business and she from teaching, but Maddy had constantly reminded the girls that she wanted them to feel they could make a home with her. However, as the couple grew older, Gerald and Maddy decided it would be better for them to live near family. "But enough about me. How have you been?" asked Beth.

"Oh, except for the occasional twinge here and there, I'm fit as a fiddle." That wasn't entirely true, of course. Gina motioned to Beth that her aunt did not hear well.

"Where's Uncle Gerald?" Beth asked a little louder than usual.

"Out on the pier fishing, where else? He lives for fishing or working on those confounded chemistry experiments. And you really don't have to shout, Beth; I'm just a little deaf in one ear." Gina pulled a face and looked away, hiding a grin.

"What's he working on now?" Beth asked. Maddy blushed and patted Beth's knee.

"I'll let him tell you," Maddy said. "Half of the pleasure of working on his projects is in sharing the plans and results with someone. I'm afraid he's taken me for granted and probably needs a new set of ears to listen to him." Just then, the sliding glass door opened again and Gerald stood there, his darkly tanned skin misted with sweat and his hands filled with speckled trout. He walked over to the sink and dumped the fish and turned to Beth.

"Can a man get a hug from his niece or am I too fishy smelling?" he asked, grinning at Beth. She walked to him and embraced him. He had taught her math, chemistry, geometry, and biology before she was old enough to take the courses in high school. Consequently, they'd formed a close bond and shared a thrill for the sciences.

"Uncle Gerald, you know I don't care about that sort of thing," she hugged him tightly. His body was warm from the sun and smelled of bait and bay water.

"Are you home to stay or will you be going back to wherever you were?" he asked as he sat on a wooden kitchen chair he'd dragged into the sitting area.

"I'm home to stay, I think," she said. Gerald smiled and took an apple cider from Gina as he sat back in the chair.

"How have you been, Uncle Gerald? It's been a long time since I've seen you. I hear you're working on some interesting experiments."

"Yes, yes I am." He looked down at his feet and looked bashful. "If you're interested, come by my lab, and I'll show you what I'm trying to create. Well, I need to get cleaned up, and you need to get some rest, little lady. You've driven a long way to get home." Gerald got up and helped Maddy to her feet. As they neared the sliding glass door, he patted Maddy on her rear and wiggled his eyebrows.

"I need to show you the results of my last experiment too, Maddy," he whispered, loud enough for her to hear and for Gina and Beth to hear as well. The two sisters smiled at each other with that knowing look.

"They're one of a kind," Gina said. "Yes they are," her sister agreed.

"You get some rest, Beth, and later we can take a walk." Beth settled into the comforter in her bedroom. She slept for so long that Gina wondered whether Beth was ill and came to the room to check on her a few times. She noticed Beth's revolver holster on the bedpost and wondered whether she had a gun under her mattress. She closed the door and let her sleep.

Later, the sisters walked up a marshy path as the warm air clung to them. The Gulf Coast was warm and humid in the early fall. But this late October night was a little cooler than expected. They dressed lightly and used mosquito spray.

"Can I talk you into remaining with me for a while?" Gina said, looking sideways at her sister.

"That would be no problem since I'm not certain what I want to do exactly. I take that back. Actually, there is a problem I'm working on." She trusted Gina to keep her confidence, as they were as close as two sisters could be. Gina would die before she betrayed her. However, she considered that it would be wise to go only so far in explaining her circumstances. She explained the mysterious disappearance of her employers and told about the man who had attacked her before she left the house on the East Coast.

"But surely you are accustomed to their being gone for a length of time considering they were mixed up in that agency business," her sister said. "They could be waiting to return."

"No, not like this. This isn't like them. They usually

make some contact with their office or with me. I haven't known them to be missing for more than a year. It's been three years now. I think they must be dead. Their daughter, Val, believes them dead, and I regret to say I had to allow her to think so."

"Could you not give her any hope?" Gina said.

"No, that would be unethical. Plus, I can't blow their cover if they are alive. I know that they had a difficult assignment, but they usually stay in touch at least digitally. But I've heard nothing. I tried tracking their devices, but nothing. The office knows nothing either."

"There isn't much you can do then, can you?" Beth looked into the distance and pondered that notion for a while. She didn't answer her sister. The silence drew out so long that Gina thought Beth had decided not to continue the conversation. Then, as they rounded a curve in the path, she spoke.

"There are a few possibilities I can check on, and I will. But it has to be done very carefully," Beth said. "Needless to say, this goes no further than the two of us."

"Like you need to ask," her sister snorted. "By the way, what happened to that handsome young man who was chasing you back east?"

"You mean Ramon." Again, Beth was silent. She pondered whether she should say anything at all. Ramon was too young for her. She was more than 10 years his senior. It wouldn't do for her to have to cope with such youthful persistence.

She looked at her sister and smiled. Gina smiled back. "Aren't you even going to give him a chance?"

"No."

2 WHEN A MAN LOVES A WOMAN

Ramon Vela was nothing if not patient and persistent. He had had a thing for Beth Larsen for years. They worked together on some projects for the agency before she was assigned to the McKeans. She was one of the brightest women he knew. Her lithe but muscled body was always at the ready. Her dark hair and dark eyes were enchanting. He had tried to get her into bed many times, but she wouldn't let him. He asked her many times why. "You're too young, Ramon. Go find some young woman you can have all to yourself. I'm not interested in young men."

"But there's only a few years difference in our ages," he said as he lay on the floor, taking a wire from her as she connected it to some other wires for a job they were doing. She checked the connection on her laptop and handed it to him. She thought she heard a sound and shushed him. It turned out to be nothing, so they left the target's space for another challenge. When they arrived at their holding place, they unloaded the equipment and checked the connection again. All was well. They did the first watch for surveillance and left when relief arrived.

He drove her to her condo and helped her inside.

When she turned and looked at him, nodding at the door, he leaned against it and folded his arms across his chest. He gave her a penetrating assessment. He looked into her eyes and then down to her breasts where they pebbled at his appraisal. She turned to walk away, and he grabbed her by the shoulders and hugged her to him, her buttocks nestled against his erection.

"Why won't you let anything grow between us, Beth?" he asked. "You know you want me. Why must you hold off like this?" She didn't answer, only shaking her head and trying to push him off, but he held her in his grip. He used one hand to turn her head toward him and brushed his lips softly against hers. Then, turning her around, he kissed her more persistently, deeper; he nudged his tongue between her lips and felt her gasp as he pushed into her mouth. His hands groped toward her bottom and pulled her into his erection.

Suddenly, he felt her push away and almost lost his balance from the force of their separation. Time had seemed to stop when he looked back at the many times he had tried to seduce her. But each time she resisted, insisting that he was too young, that she was too old. Nonsense. She just needed the right incentive, and he knew he could find it. She wasn't an ice maiden. It was easy to check on the background of colleagues in the service, especially if you knew the right people. He knew a guy who knew a guy.

Before long, he found that she was just a brainy woman who threw herself into her work. She was recruited straight from college into the service and trained for the rigors of the work. As the technical world changed, she changed with it, soaking up and absorbing everything the government wanted her to learn. She was a walking encyclopedia, with a talent for electronic and digital work and the strength of vision and nerve to shoot when necessary. Fortunately, the service saw her value as an egghead instead of as a field agent, and she escaped most of the dangerous assignments for background work. Was she happy with that? He wanted to know, but getting her to open up to him was one of the most challenging things he'd ever done.

He arrived at Beth's sister's doorstep weeks after she'd settled in to a life of consulting and teaching. She had a knack for testing out of any university's program to quickly get any degree she wanted, so her decision to teach did not surprise him. The sun was going down when he reached her home; it had been a warm day, but the cool of the evening was gathering. He knocked on the door and rang the doorbell. Before long, he heard footsteps and someone shuffling toward the door. A woman in an orange gauzy dress stood there looking at him as though he had grown two heads.

"I'm looking for Beth Larsen," he said. "I understand she lives here." The woman stood there for a moment. She looked so much like Beth that he might have mistaken the sister for Beth. They were identical twins; people who did not know them often mistook one for the other. However, Ramon knew instantly that this was not Beth but her sister, Gina.

"Who should I say is calling?" she asked, pursing her lips as though she were someone's old tia. "My sister is indisposed at the moment."

"What, is she washing her hair or something?" Just then, a woman dressed in a white robe came up behind the one who answered the door. Her head was wrapped in a towel and the robe covered her from head to foot. He knew it was her as he spied her beautiful, smooth legs. He could feel himself growing hard.

"As a matter of fact, I am," Beth beamed at him. "Well, don't just stand there, come on in." He bounced up the steps like an eager teenager.

They moved into the living room and Gina stood to the side as Beth pulled the towel from her head and let it drop to a nearby table. She was beautiful, Ramon decided. That moment took his breath away. She was all freshness and squeaky-clean exuberance. Her eyes glittered as she assessed him. He could feel her appraisal of his body. Likewise, he was imagining what she looked like under that big fluffy robe. He felt himself get painfully hard when she finally came toward him with her hand outstretched.

"Ramon, I'm so surprised to see you," she said, as though she were out of breath. "How did you find me? What are you doing here?" He smiled and looked at Beth's sister as though waiting for her to give them some privacy before he spoke. Gina took the hint and motioned to the kitchen, saying she would get something for them to drink. Beth's eyes roamed over his broad shoulders and his muscled chest, quite apparent under his tight fitting T-shirt. She was heading for his waist when he spoke; her eyes met his flashing hazel eyes.

"I looked you up, of course," he said. "You know that there is nowhere you can go that I can't find." She was still holding her hand out and instead of shaking her hand, he pulled her into an embrace. "Oh!" she said. Her robe fell open a bit and he saw a tantalizing view of her plump breasts. This was getting too painful. He released her as she looked down and realized her robe revealed a little more than she thought.

"Um, can you give me a moment, Ramon? I'm going to change. Have a seat while I'm away. Be back in a snap."

She rushed to the hallway that led to her rooms to change. When she returned, a short tight jean skirt showed off her plump bottom and a pink T-shirt did little to hide her perky breasts. She brushed her hair back from her face, hair escaping from a messy ponytail. Soft beige leather sandals hugged her slender feet. He took a deep breath as he took her in and realized he needed to gain her trust, so he forced his mind to safer ground. He stood near a high table with pictures of her sister and her family as well as pictures of her and her parents. He smiled as she walked toward him; he pointed at one of the family photos.

"Your folks?" he asked.

"Yes, my parents with me and my sister." A long period of silence followed as she appeared to be going down memory lane, thinking of the past. Her eyes tore away from the framed photograph and back at him. "My parents died in an accident when we were children." He knew that. Over the years, they had shared little confidences, her parents' early death, her fear of large bodies of water, but seeing her engage in the emotions while surrounded by familial belongings, within her own environment, was different.

"It's good that you have family still here," he said. "We tend to forget how important that is while we're at the business of protecting the country." He wanted to say something else, something that would impress her, but the words just didn't come. There was quiet in the house. The sister must have gone out, he thought. Beth turned and went to the kitchen where the drinks had been left on a counter top. Hmmm. Considerate sister. She set the tray down on a glass coffee table, handed him a glass of iced tea and invited him to sit on the couch with her.

"What brings you this way, Ramon?" she asked. "I thought you were on assignment."

"I was, but I made some decisions recently. I decided to go into semi-retirement."

"What does 'semi-retirement' mean? And how could that be? You're too young." He stiffened at that comment, but tried to relax so as not to get into a battle of wills with her. Actually, he had invested his income handily. That, along with his share of the family business, made it possible for him to invest wisely. As a result, he never had to work if he didn't want to do so. But, he didn't want her to know that he had millions. It would turn her off and make her think he was trying to buy her love. Not true. He wanted her to want him, just for himself and for what he saw in her.

"It means that I'll do jobs for the service if they need someone to fill in, but essentially, I'm a free man." She sat there for a while looking as though she was trying to figure out why he had done that. Her chocolate brown eyes looked into his hazel eyes. He could feel himself falling deeper in love with her. He also felt himself aching with arousal. It was always this way when he saw her. He hoped she didn't notice. Convincing her to take him seriously would be tough if he let her know that his attraction to her was on such a basic sensual level.

"Are you looking for work then?" she asked.

"No." He paused, not sure how much to tell her.

"Beth, I don't need the money actually. I saved when I worked and have some money from family investments. I live on money generated from my investments, and my family owns a chain of restaurants. And," he hesitated, watching for her facial reactions, "I have other options, investments." She looked at him as though he were some odd, Big Foot character, sipped from her glass and then coughed into her hand.

"Um, right. So, what are you doing here?"

"I'm here to see you, Beth."

Moments ticked by. The tension was so thick that he was nearly desperate to think of something to say, but again his words caught in his throat and his tongue felt swollen, his mouth dry. His cock swelled, growing harder as he struggled to maintain control. Finally, he realized that she was afraid, maybe not of him, but of change. She had moved here to make a change in her life, and now he was pushing her too fast, again. Pushing her to realize that he wanted her to make a change for him.

"I … I mean, I am here to see you, but I have a place in the area and wanted to know if you'd be interested in going to dinner or something, going dancing, whatever it is that you like to do here." They had gone out with some of the people they worked with back east, but it was always impersonal. His words died as he saw her frown. She put a hand to her face and smoothed a hand on her jean skirt, then smiled brightly, as though she couldn't think of what else to do. He could see the nipples of her breasts through her pink shirt. She licked her lips. He held his breath, becoming painfully aroused but not wanting her to know.

"You came all this way so we could date?" she asked.

"No, I have family in the area. I always have. You know that, Beth." She took a moment to review what she knew of him, realizing in that instant that he was more at home than she was. "Right, I'm glad you came by, Ramon. I'd like to go out to dinner with you. But, I'm not really dating."

"Oh, I'm not asking for a date or anything like that." Liar. "I just want us to be friends, just friends." It sounded weak; his words were faltering. He was lying to her. He could never get his thoughts straight around this woman. How could he possibly convince her he was serious if he couldn't come up with a better excuse than that? He had pondered this dilemma for a while. He knew that she might think that his hormones drove him, but the truth was, when they were together, they never lacked for things to talk about and never tired of one another's company. There was something about being with her that filled an emptiness in him. The plush beige carpet seemed to offer some comfort to his feet, as he shifted toward her on the couch.

"The truth, Beth, is I really want to see whether we can be closer than friends. All these years we've worked together have been difficult for me. You know that I've always felt something for you. You know that. We've talked about it."

"I know," she said.

"You know!" his voice croaking and throat tightening. He felt some relief but was still tense. At least she was admitting to being aware of how he felt.

"Yes, I know, but as I told you before, Ramon, you should be looking to date someone your own age or younger." He had had it then. All his control broke in that moment. He reached for her and dragged her onto his lap, placed a hand on the back of her head and tilted her mouth to him. His kiss was light and teasing at first and then his lips pressed against hers with insistence. He groaned. She mewled. He could feel her pebbled nipples through the thin fabric of her shirt as he moved his hands up and down her arm and then on one breast. He squeezed gently. She shivered, but he could tell it was not because she was cold. He realized in that moment that he had to show her that there was no real difference in them. That he could satisfy her. Age made no difference in the bed or otherwise for that matter. He held her firmly and placed a hand on her knee, gentling her. She inhaled sharply, tensing as though she planned to escape.

"Easy, easy, chica" he murmured. He massaged her knee lightly, then increased pressure gradually and smoothed his way up to the inside of her thighs. He continued to kiss her, pressing on her lips and pulling away, pushing his tongue into her mouth to let her know what he wanted to do to her. When he made contact with her tongue, she flinched again as though she would pull away from him, and he held her firmly in place. When she began to relax, he made his way further up her thigh to the apex of her sex where he discovered a surprise. No underwear! She was naked under there.

He almost came the moment he realized she was not only naked but moist. He placed a finger in the folds of her pussy and circled lightly. She moaned and shivered again. The sound of her deep voice made him so hard that he had to think of something to pull himself back from the edge. He found her clitoris and circled it, then placed two fingers in her sex and a thumb on her clitoris. She arched her back, and it didn't take long. She stiffened and shattered in his arms, her pussy contracting around his fingers.

Suddenly, she pulled away from him and plopped on the couch beside him. She panted, her eyes wide. He breathed deeply. She finally looked at him with that look, turning her head slightly to the side. That look that said she understood what he was feeling and that she felt some of what he was trying to say physically that he couldn't say with words. With one hand, she smoothed her hair from her face and took a deep breath, shivering a bit at the physical revelation. She hadn't been touched like that in a long time, maybe not ever. It had been a long time since she'd had sex; a long time since a man had touched her like this, brought her to a climax. She remembered the embrace that they'd shared on the job some years back, but this was different, quite different. Moments passed as she struggled to collect herself. She left the living room and returned with a warm washcloth and a hand towel. He used it and pulled her down beside him again. This time, she sat on the far side of the couch.

"Ramon, I, I think I understand what you're wanting. But um. I can't." She tried to create some emotional and physical distance between them. She was tempted to allow him to continue his pursuit, but somehow it felt wrong. She couldn't allow him to waste his life on her. She had to make him see that he needed to find someone his own age. She wanted a family, but not like this. He would have expectations that she could not meet.

"It's not just that, and you know it, Beth. Don't insult me. I've been running after you for a long time. It's time to stop saying no all the time and give me a chance. Just a chance. That's all I'm asking. Can't we just see whether it can develop? Can't you just keep an open mind?" How could she keep putting up this wall between them when he'd just given her a gift?

"Running after me?" she said incredulously. "You

have not been running after me! I would never have allowed you to do that."

"It's a figure of speech, Beth. I've been trying to convince you to give us a chance for years. Don't pretend you don't know," he said, with an angry tinge to his voice.

She took a deep breath and looked at him with an air of resignation. It was risky to get involved with Ramon; he was a handsome man, six feet of all male, muscled and broad shouldered. The women were always giving him a second look. His dark, good looks were cause for any woman to want to be with Ramon, but that was just the problem. A. He was too young. B. He was too attractive. Men who knew they were attractive had an excessive amount of confidence and little motivation to be faithful. But, if he had waited this long just for a chance to date her, why not? The orgasm he had just given her suggested he had experience beyond his late 20s. Maybe it was time to explore this. It had been a long time since she had had sex. The orgasm he had given her suggested that he was able to restrain himself, to give his partner pleasure before thinking of his own.

Her first lover had been callous and selfish, delivering pain but no satisfaction. She'd given up on sex and decided that dating was OK, but sex was out. For years, she buried herself in her work, not giving a thought to it. She had everything she wanted in the McKeans' household. She could play mother to Val and have the dream of a family without the financial and emotional hassles. But lately, she wondered whether she had made a mistake. Life was passing her by.

"OK, but let's take it slow. Can we? I mean. I appreciate your enthusiasm, but understand that I can't go fast. I need to take my time." Ramon had come into her life, giving her unmistakable hints of his affection. He'd been like a puppy at first, annoying but sweet. It wasn't difficult to dismiss him from her heart and mind when they were on the job far away in the cold north. When she thought back to her early bad experience with sex, she shivered. She didn't want to take a chance again; to risk getting hurt, both physically and emotionally. Her first lover only wanted sex; she had thought it was more than that. When she discovered her mistake, she slammed the door closed to her heart and vowed never to trust a man again. But Ramon was nothing if not determined. She realized that he would need to have a fair chance before he'd be convinced that she could not make a commitment to him. Maybe if he had a chance to see how it would be with her, he would change his mind.

"Shall I pick you up tomorrow at say 7?" he asked. She nodded. He stood and hugged her again. Kissed her briefly on the lips and turned to leave.

3 THREE IS A CROWD

Arnold Dickens wondered what it would take to get to the codes that the daft woman had on her computer. He wanted to break into the woman's home, but the last man who'd done that was never found. It was tricky getting access to devices in a house that was well guarded; however, he had worked on it for quite some time.

He wanted to get back at the smartass who made a life with her, Ramon. Beth and some of her friends had been in New York for a night on the town when Arnold happened to be picking up some protection money from a client who owned a nightclub. He stopped at the bar for a drink when he saw this looker of a woman, with a sweet oval face and dark hair. He listened for a while and picked up bits and pieces of names. There was something about her that made him want to throw her over his shoulder, take her to his condo and fuck her for days. But the smartass man she was with had squared up with him.

There weren't many people who could get the best of him. He was at least six feet with broad shoulders and muscled thighs and arms. No one messed with Arnold Dickens; not only was he big, but he was smart. He had made money making sure that some New York merchants were well protected from people like him. But the other thugs were not as smart as him. He grinned, thinking back on the way he had found the chick; he had been waiting for the right time to fuck her.

Usually, men took one look at him, assumed he was a marine and walked away. But not this kid who was with her that night. Arnold outweighed the kid, but the kid was quick and strong. He'd tapped Arnold on the shoulder and did something to his neck that let Arnold know that the asshole was a professional.

He had been sitting in his car tailing Beth one day when some man got into his car. Arnold was surprised because he was usually careful.

"Don't look at me," the man said. "Keep looking forward." He could tell the man had a gun, though he couldn't see it. "Don't say anything. There's money in it for you if you do what I say." A few seconds passed and the man pulled out a bundle of money. He set it on the seat between them. Arnold's eyes bulged at the amount of money on the seat.

"We know you're keeping an eye on the woman, Beth," he said. "You can do with her what you want, but we want you to use this." He handed Arnold a travel drive.

"If you can get close enough to plug this in, we'll pay you a lot more than what you see on the seat between us," he said. "We know who you are. We know who your relatives and friends are." The man began ticking off names.

"If you try to find us, you and your family are dead. We only want you to do this job. There's more in it for you if you manage to get what we need."

"How will I know what I'm looking for?" Arnold asked. "I don't know anything about computers. I'm just." Shit! He wondered what the hell he'd gotten himself into.

"We know," the man said. "If you need help, we'll find you. We know every step you're taking. Just plug this drive into the devices. We'll do the rest."

Arnold found out by working with some of his underground contacts that the McKeans, who had worked for the agency, had gone overseas. They were an odd pair. No one could tell that they weren't Arabs as they had the perfect dark coloring. But somewhere, they must have fucked up because they had never come back to their home.

It wouldn't take long for him to check out her computer himself if he could just get to it. Maybe she was hiding what the man wanted somewhere obvious on the computer. Maybe she had whatever the man wanted on some other device. But it was taking too long. He waited impatiently. He knew he could get to her if he could just get her alone. She was dangerous. But he liked them like that. The fuck was better. He liked to get a woman alone, tie her up and make her scream for his cock. He took himself in hand thinking about the hot woman who thought she was smarter than he was. He would show her. She wouldn't be able to hide for much longer. That pesky boyfriend of hers who kept sniffing around her ass would need to be eliminated. He could take care of both of them. Just thinking of it made him come. He licked his lips as he left the area. He would get this sweet puss and make her tell him where the codes were.

Ramon drove the 30 miles from his brother's house in League City to Galveston, immersed in thought: how best to convince Beth to take him seriously. She knew the basics about his origins. He wondered whether his family background might be part of what made her hesitant to get involved with him. Something in him wanted to take care of her; to give her everything she wanted, to keep her safe.

Some women did not like getting involved with younger men. He was the youngest in a large family. They had been poor. Early in their family life, his mother worked from dawn to dusk, cleaning houses, making food to sell at offices and doing other small jobs. His father, Nicolas, worked along with his brother, Diego, as a cook in a restaurant. Finally, the two brothers opened their own restaurant. They were able to run the restaurant with Nicolas' wife, Francisca, and some hired help at first.

As the children became old enough to work, they came home after school to work in the family business. They went to school like other children, and came home to set tables, clear tables, sweep floors, and help get orders to customers. Ramon's older sisters and brothers were always there, tugging him from place to place. Isabella and Nicolito, the two oldest siblings, had it the hardest, always taking over for his parents, being the parents while their parents worked. The younger ones, Rosa, Alejandro and Mateo, were rebellious to a point. Their parents reminded them that it was important to respect the sacrifice their elders made on their behalf and to work hard.

Years ago, before Ramon was born, their father, Nicolas, had driven the family from San Antonio to Houston for work. Though his parents had some work in San Antonio, it wasn't enough for the growing family. Nicolas and his wife, Francisca, lived in San Antonio during their early marriage, marrying young. They had lived in San Antonio all of their lives as had many generations of their family members before them. Many people asked from where they came. Nicolas and Francisca always smiled and looked at them blankly because they were from the U.S.; their family and their family before them were simply on the land before any Europeans came, way before the Mayflower. The family was one of thousands of Spanish-speaking natives of Texas who had settled near the missions of San Antonio.

Before Ramon was old enough to walk, his sister, Rosa, taught him to speak and read in Spanish and English. The words made sense to him. He heard his parents and siblings throwing words back and forth when he was a toddler. He heard them speak a different language to the customers, English, and Spanish to each other. However, every now and then, they spoke to each other in English too. It wasn't long before he could write and do sums in his head. He sat beside his older sister, Isabella, while she added up long columns of numbers for his parents, doing the bookkeeping, the ordering of supplies and food for the restaurant and generally making certain that everything was running smoothly.

She always gave him a treat of some sort, an egg and bacon burrito or sopapillas, drenched in cinnamon and butter. While Isabella taught him everything about math and numbers, Rosa taught him languages. His brother Alejandro was the science expert and helped him understand everything from astronomy to biology. His brother Mateo introduced him to computers; the two of them were closest in age and worked on coding and software. The sisters and brothers worked with him every chance they got. He was the youngest, their parents' surprise baby.

Before he was old enough to get to the third grade, he was bored with school and began to cause trouble in class. So it was no surprise to his siblings that he was quick to pass tests, although he was unable to content himself with going quietly through the grades while he waited for the other students to catch up. His parents shook their heads and warned his brothers and sisters to let him have a normal childhood, but his thirst for learning was unquenchable. And his sisters and brothers thought it was cute to make him a little Einstein. As the youngest, he was accustomed to being around older people. It felt natural.

He couldn't imagine life without his family. His sisters, brothers and his mother and father were everything. Still, he wasn't interested in the restaurant business, not to the extent his family was. He could cook and enjoyed it; he could run a restaurant. He was sure of it; he grew up around it. It was second nature. But, in the long run, it wasn't what he wanted to do with his life. He wanted to see the world; he wanted adventure; he wanted a chance to see whether running a restaurant was all there was. It turned out it wasn't. At the insistence of his sister Isabella, he was able to test out of most grades. His parents insisted that he attend at least a few.

He graduated from high school by the time he was 14 and college by the time he was 17. As a result of his test scores, he was on the government's radar before he turned 18. When he took all the tests the government had, the recruiters found that his scores were nearly perfect and approached him about undercover work. Some of what he did was quite beneath his capabilities, but once he was assigned to work with Ethel Elizabeth Larsen, there was no place else he wanted to be. For Ramon, it was love at first sight, maybe second and third as well. Beth had no idea. He recalled those times when the two of them relaxed together at the McKeans', cooking their favorite dishes and perusing his latest gardening experiments. She enjoyed doing things with him. The problem was she didn't want to admit it.

Ramon pulled up in his BMW five minutes before their date was to begin. He had taken great care with his appearance, making certain he was dressed to fit in on the island but to appeal to Beth as well. His black twill pants and dark shirt were crisp and pressed. He wore dark boat shoes; he took one more look at himself before ringing the doorbell. There was no answer for a time. The sun was setting to the west, pelicans soared overhead and white egrets stepped gingerly through the marsh water in the flat expanse of wet inlets across from Gina's house. Gina and Beth lived on a remote stretch of road on the bay side of the west end of island. The house sat on tall pilings to protect it from high water during tropical storms. The water from the bay lapped on the shore, a quiet respite from the bustle of the nearby city. This was much better than the city life in which he'd grown up.

The door slid open to a radiant Beth, dressed in lavender colors and flowing folds. He took a deep breath as he pored over her soft skin. Her long hair was pulled back in a messy assortment of dark curls. Her silver jewelry glistened, highlighting her glittering chocolate eyes. She licked her upper lip, moist with coral color. He could feel himself grow hard at the gesture. Her perky breasts pebbled under her gauzy clothes. She was a knockout.

"Sweetheart, maybe we should go inside and explore that exceptional attire you're wearing," he said, smiling at her. She smirked.

"This is supposed to be a date, Ramon, not a seduction," she said, rounding him and moving down the steps. He turned and stared at her luscious buttocks; his aching cock was not behaving. He tried to think of something else, looking off into the distance into the bay. He counted backward from 100. When he realized she was standing beside his black BMW SUV, he walked down the steps and opened the door for her.

"I made a reservation for us at Orleans," he said. "I hope that meets your approval."

"I haven't been home in so long, I wouldn't know where to have dinner," she said. "However, the restaurant is on The Strand, so it should be fun." He knew that the view from one of the restaurants near the piers would be more romantic for any other woman, but not for Beth because of her fear of large bodies of water.

They drove along in silence for a while before Ramon cleared his throat and broached the subject of the shooting. "Have you given any more thought to what happened at the McKeans'?"

She looked out the window, and he kicked himself for asking. This wasn't exactly the most romantic conversation to have on a date. He had promised himself they would not talk about work, but here he was breaking the promise.

"Honestly, I've tried not to think about it, but you're right to bring it up. Obviously, something's not right with the McKeans' disappearance. I've been doing a little research on their last assignment."

"Oh, I thought that was highly classified and impossible to get to once you're retired," he said as he made a left onto Stewart Road. Of course, he knew better; anything was accessible for the right price or if you knew the right people or the right method of access.

"There are ways and then there are ways," she said, turning away from him as she watched the fields of cattle. "I haven't given up the notion of finding out what happened to them. I have a friend who might be able to help me." Beth explained that she had contacted one of her many covert net friends to see whether she could help her find out more. So far, not much had been unearthed.

"It's possible they survived their last assignment, but Beth, do you really think it's wise to explore the possibility?" he asked. "Maybe what's hidden should stay hidden. You already have been the object of an attempted murder." Beth sighed deeply.

"Yes, I know, but I can't give it up. We really don't know if that attempt was aimed at us or at the McKeans — whether whoever it was that sent that assassin was after them or us." She let a few minutes pass by. Ramon pressed a button to turn on the XM station. His jaw tightened as he considered her words.

"If you could have seen the look on Val's face when she perused her parent's belongings, you would understand," Beth said. Val had been part of their duties. The McKeans' daughter had had a nanny and attended boarding school most of the time, but her parents hired Ramon and the agency kept Beth nearby too. With freelancing from the agency and the McKeans' fees, he had become financially comfortable.

Ramon didn't respond to Beth's assertion that she

could not just leave the case alone. He gritted his teeth, continuing to drive, turning left on 61st Street and then right on Broadway. At the first stoplight, he looked at her and realized they were letting work get in the way of a romantic evening. He reached to her and squeezed her hand gently.

"Let's not give that any thought just yet, Beth," he said. "It's time you and I enjoyed a little of what life has to offer besides work." She gave him a tremulous smile and smoothed hair back from her face.

Taking a deep breath, she said, "Yes, yes, you're right. It's time to enjoy living for a while. Time to put this … this angst behind us at least for a time."

He grinned at her. "That's my girl." She laughed at him. "Girl?" she asked.

He reached for her elbow and brought her over to him. He put an arm around her shoulders. "Yes," he said, with that little bit of a Spanish dialect. "Chica, you're always a girl to me." She smiled.

Maddy and Gerald Armstrong had long given up the notion of having children when Maddy's sister died in a boating accident with her husband. The two sisters, Beth and Gina, were twins and had a bond that was close — just like the bond between Maddy and her twin Emma. When Emma died, it seemed a hole had grown where Maddy's heart was. At the time, she and Gerald were living in a middle-class neighborhood in League City. The house was paid for, and she and Gerald had always had plenty of cash. He'd saved his money and sold a couple of his inventions. When it was clear that Emma's girls had nowhere to go, Maddy and Gerald invited the children to move in with them. It was a salve for Maddy's heart. Every day that the girls were with her, she saw glimpses of her own sister in the twins. It seemed that before long they were grown up, going on dates and moving out of the house. She missed them when they were gone. So when Gina's husband died, it seemed like the natural thing for Maddy and Gerald to move next door. Of course, it was at Gina's invitation. They could have moved to a posh seniors village, but being near family seemed more important.

Gina was right, of course. As the months and years passed, after Gina's husband died, Maddy and Gina formed a special friendship. The heat of the Gulf was a bit too much for Maddy during the summer, but when it became unbearable, she and Gerald went north to Canada. But lately, she felt a need to be near the girls. Something didn't feel quite right about Beth's sudden reappearance. Maddy had always prided herself on knowing the two girls better than anyone else. It seemed to her that Beth was restless and that Gina had simply given up on finding another great love. Maddy's intuition told her something or someone dangerous was lurking about. She called her friends in the neighborhood sometime after Beth had arrived and found that a strange looking man had moved in on the marshy side of the road, in that little brown house that the owners neglected so.

Maddy's friend, Alice, was ever suspicious too, and the two nosy ladies kept an eye on everything that happened. They noted every car — make and model — that drove down Sportsman's Road, along with the license plate numbers, if they could get them. Over the years, it became a sort of perverse hobby. It was on one of those days that Gerald decided to try out his latest chemical experiment.

"What are you up to now?" Maddy asked as she walked into the small space he had turned into a laboratory.

"Ah, wouldn't you like to know?" he asked, wiggling his bushy eyebrows. "It's a secret."

"If it's so much of a secret, why did you let the girls think you'd tell them?" she asked, getting up to look at one of the slides under his microscope.

"Careful with that, my dear," he said, moving a small vial out of the way of her elbow.

"Gerald, did you notice that some man moved in across the street?" she asked. He was busy studying his notes and turning a cage around so he could study the mice in it. He gave one of them another taste of the concoction and then allowed the mouse into the cage with the other. The mouse that had been given the special brew mounted the female mouse and had a quick time of it. Maddy's eyebrows rose.

"What are you doing?" she asked, looking from the mice to Gerald.

"I've created an aphrodisiac for us, my dear," he said, smiling. "Would you care to try some?"

"I don't know, Gerald," she said backing away. "Are you sure it's safe?" She had been something of a chemistry student herself. They had met in a high school chemistry class where she had set the lab ablaze along with Gerald's pants. She'd helped him out of them, and the class had applauded her bravery. It was love at first explosion for them.

"Of course it's safe. There's a different formula for me and a different one for you. Yours has some secret ingredients, along with Astragalus, a little Black Cohosh, and ginseng. And mine has False Unicorn, Fo Ti, and ginseng, along with some special other blends. Taste yours," he said, handing her a champagne flute. He smiled as she took the glass from him and drank the concoction down. He then drank his. They grinned at each other and made their way into the bedroom.

While Gerald slept the bliss of a satisfied man, Maddy got up to use the bathroom and noticed that the sliding glass door to Gina's house was open, as was their own sliding glass door, which led to the decks between the two houses. She thought that was strange since she was certain she had locked her own door. She knew that Gina would never leave the door open. She walked into the living room and looked around. Nothing seemed out of place, but she heard a sound coming from Gerald's laboratory. Using her cane, she walked to the faux fireplace and grabbed a poker. She walked to the door of the lab and looked inside. She could see the silhouette of a man who appeared to be searching through Gerald's desk drawer. The crackling of paper and shuffling of folders hid her stealthy approach. She walked silently up behind the man and whacked him over the back. He fell to the floor, stunned; she turned on the light on the desk and pulled the ski mask from his head and gave him a good look. He had some computer travel drives in his hand. She grabbed them out of his hand and ran to the bathroom, screaming: "Gerald, get up. There's an intruder in the house."

It was just her luck that Gerald was so insensate and so sated that he would sleep through anything, even this. She realized that she was on her own, as she locked the bathroom door. The doorknob was small and flimsy and hadn't been changed in a decade, so it rattled each time the user pulled the door shut. She knew it would not hold against someone who wanted to get in. It didn't take long for the intruder to recover and make his way to the bathroom. Maddy looked around the small bathroom for another weapon. In her excitement, she'd dropped the poker. Now, she'd locked herself in the bathroom and she could hear the man turning the knob on the door.

"Let me in, you old bat," he said, loud enough for her to hear, but not so loud that it would wake up Gerald.

"Gerald, you old Phart! Wake up!" She screamed. Nothing. Gerald slept peacefully. The man continued to rattle the door. In a panic, Maddy grabbed the only thing she could lift to use as a weapon, the top of the toilet bowl. It was heavy ceramic. The devil wrenched off the fragile doorknob and was pushing the door open. She stood behind the door. When his head came through the door, she brought the lid down on him as hard as she could.

4 THE DATE

They ate at Orleans restaurant on The Strand. As they left
the restaurant, they walked past the Tall Ship Elissa,
anchored to the pier in the distance. Tourists wandered in
and out of the ship, and dolphins swam out in the harbor.
Large brown pelicans perched on the many thick pier posts.
The sun was quickly setting. After a satisfying dinner of
lobster and salad, with bread pudding for dessert, they
enjoyed sipping wine and beer. When they left the
restaurant, they walked west on The Strand and stopped at
the Galveston Arts Center, where an installation of abstract
art and ancient bells was housed. Hundreds of tourists
weaved in and out of traffic and darted into quaint shops
illuminated by street lamps and shop lights.

They were about to cross a street to a creamery on the
west end of The Strand when Beth felt someone shove her
from behind into the path of a passing car. Before she
could fall, Ramon reached out a long arm and scooped her
up to him. It was dark by then, and people gasped as they
watched what had happened. A woman pointed to a man
running down the street back toward the harbor. Ramon
held Beth tight, realizing that this near miss was intentional

and that he should stay nearby. He carried a weapon on him but could see no point in chasing the man. He was long gone and it was too dark to see where the man went. He could feel her heart beating like the heart of a bird held tightly in the grip of a predator. He soothed her, running a hand down her back and whispering endearing words to her.

"It's OK, mi vida," he said, realizing with a chill that she was his life, his world. "It will be all right. I'll catch the son of a. …" He realized he didn't want to curse and bit back the expletive.

Beth shook with a surge of adrenaline. She took deep breaths, realizing that she needed to get herself in a quiet space to regroup. Her weapon was inconveniently in her purse. Obviously, whoever was threatened by her search for the McKeans wanted her to stop. This was a warning. Ramon led her to a restaurant and asked for a table. It was dark and quiet inside. When a waiter approached, Ramon ordered cognac and water, explaining that his wife had had an upset and they simply wanted to collect themselves before moving on. Beth looked at him with a raised eyebrow. His mouth twitched with amusement as they waited for the man to return with their drinks.

"Taking a bit of liberty, aren't you?" she asked.

"It makes me feel good to take care of you, Beth. Do you mind if I think of you in that way? It's the way I have felt for years. You can't change my mind. Besides, you need me and you know it."

The drinks came, and they both sipped, allowing time to pass.

"I'm in no condition to argue with you," she said. "If you hadn't caught me, I would be no more."

"Let's don't think about that," he said. "I've got a room at the Tremont for tonight. Would you like to join me?" She looked at him, stunned that he had planned for them to be together. The Tremont was one of the best hotels in Galveston. He would want to impress her by taking her there. But she did not intend to go to his room.

"I think it would be better for me to go home," she said, taking a deep breath.

"Home to your sister?" he asked, smiling at her. "Could it be that you're afraid to be alone with me, Beth, mi querida, my dear?"

She looked at him and turned her head, focusing on some spot in the distance. It was probably a good idea not to return just now. However, what if someone were at Gina's house? Would Gina be OK? Also, how could she justify being with Ramon after what happened in the street? She might be dragging him into this without need. Besides, there was the issue of his age. How young was he anyway? She sighed.

"Beth, I can see the wheels turning in your mind. You need to let go of this idea that you are alone on this search for the McKeans. I'm in it with you. As for my age, which I know you're thinking of and hesitating about, does it really matter in the long run, Beth? If I were a teenager, that might be different, but I'm not, and you're not. We're two adults." She took another deep breath and shivered, clutching her hands in her lap. He reached for her hand and smoothed his thumb over her wrist. She could feel her breasts getting full from just that one little gesture.

"Beth, I won't push you further than you want to go," he whispered. "But you need someone to hold you tonight." She realized he was right. It was useless to argue, but something told her things were not peaceful at home.

"Let me call my sister and aunt to be certain they're OK and to warn them to invite a friend over to stay the night," she said. She took out her cell phone and walked to the front of the restaurant where she called her sister. There was no answer, so she left a message letting Gina know to be on guard and that she might be out for most of the night. She added that it might be a good idea for Gina to spend the night with a friend. When she came back to the table, Ramon rose from his seat, respectfully, and helped her sit in her chair by pulling it out for her. When she was settled in at the table again, he looked at her with one eyebrow arched as though asking her whether she was ready.

She nodded. He said nothing and helped her gather her belongings and head out the door. It was a short walk to the hotel. When they arrived at the same corner where she was pushed, he put his arm around her and led her down the steps to the street. No cars were crossing the street then. The clothing store on the corner was lit with unusual decorations. The souvenir shop across the street flashed garish lights in red and blue. They crossed the red-bricked street. He helped her up the curb at the opposite side and walked on to the end of the corner, near the Mardi Gras arch, which was there year-round, and into the hotel entrance.

A trio of musicians played in the lobby: a horn player, a pianist and a bass player. The Electric Harmony group filled the expansive room with mellow sounds. Beth could feel herself calming down; Ramon motioned to a seat in the lobby and they sat near one another listening to the music. Ramon placed a proprietary arm around her shoulders but continued to peruse the room. They faced the musicians and the entrance so he had a good view of whoever came in. Noting nothing extraordinary about the families and couples who entered, he began to relax. A waitress brought drinks, and they sat for an hour, content with the calm atmosphere. When Beth leaned her head on his shoulder, he knew it was time to leave. He led her up to his room, opened the door and took her small purse from her. He opened the small refrigerator and poured water into a glass. She drank it and offered him back the glass. He didn't want to say anything lest the mood be broken. The sexual tension was so thick he could taste it. He breathed in her light apple like perfume.

Her beauty was so dazzling; he felt he might never get enough of her. Her perky breasts beaded through her thin gauzy top. He walked the short two steps to her and placed his hands on her shoulders. She was shorter, but not by much. He placed his hands on her cheeks and kissed her, softly pressing his lips to hers. Beth could feel herself become aroused, but she fought it. It was difficult to do so. He was so handsome. He was dressed in black twill pants that hung low on his slim hips. His dark striped shirt was unbuttoned at the top, showing a dusting of dark hair. His broad shoulders were muscled under his clothing. His dark hair was swept back from his face. He smelled of bergamot and spice. She reached up to clasp his arms as he kissed her and felt the hardness of his arm muscles. He pulled her into him and she felt his erection, hard and large. His chest expanded as he took a deep breath and looked into her chocolate eyes.

"Beth?" She nodded.

She was so gorgeous, and he was so hard. He thought he might lose it before he got her clothes off. He would make this good for her. He would not be like some young schoolboy, coming before she could be satisfied. She would never say no to him again. So he slowed himself down, thought of her, of her pleasure, of what she would be feeling. He sat her on the bed and ran his hand down her arms. He then knelt at her feet and took off first one sandal and then the other. He sat cross-legged on the floor and put one of her feet in his lap. He began to massage it slowly, working his thumbs and fingers into the tendons of her foot, slowly, but firmly rubbing each toe, between her toes and running a finger down the middle of her foot and to the heel. He massaged deeply at the ball of her foot and into the arch of her foot. She moaned with pleasure, and the sound of her made him harden even more.

He ran his hands up her legs and hooked a finger into her underwear, drawing the lacy article slowly down her legs. He tossed the panties on the dresser behind him and spread her legs open. He smoothed his hands up her thighs, kneading them gently. When he reached her center, her wetness coated his fingers. She panted and looked down at him as he reached up to her. He placed a finger in her wetness and licked it. She took a deep breath and leaned on her hands, her head back. He pulled the skirt she wore off her hips and then untied the strings of her blouse and lifted it off over her head. She wore no bra; her small, plump breasts sat up, the nipples hard and needy. She tried to cover her breasts with one hand and he moved her hand away, impatient and incredulous that she would want to cover such beauty.

"My god, you are gorgeous," he said, standing to get a better look at her. She gave a shy smile and looked away. He quickly divested himself of his pants, shirt and underclothes. He sat on the bed with her. He didn't want to frighten her with the force of his passion, so he took another deep breath and tried to think of numbers, anything, to slow himself down and focus on her pleasure. He'd left the light on in the bathroom to give himself enough light to see her. The dew of her arousal coated the tender tissues of her sex. Her hooded clitoris sat erect and pearly. "I want to see you, touch you," he said in a raspy voice.

"I want to see you too," she said, marveling at the hard rippling plane of his stomach and his broad chest. He was simply beautiful. The muscles of his calves were large and well developed; his thigh muscles turned slightly where the tendons showed a thickness and strength that made her stomach flip. His erection was large and long, the tip glistening with his seminal fluid. He was breathing deeply as he took in her voluptuous curves. Where he was hard, she was soft. He reached for her and turned her head toward him to take her mouth in another soul-wrenching kiss. He pulled her up as though she weighed nothing and laid her back on the bed. He nestled beside her, giving her a chance to touch him. He cupped her breast, fingering her nipple and pinching it gently. He kissed her breast, each one, going from one to the other as though he were holding them in deep reverence. The dusty rose nipples sat at attention. He licked them and she jumped. "You like that," he said, a statement rather than a question. Then, he began to suckle her breasts, pulling on them, licking and sucking until she could take no more.

"Ramon, please," she said. He chuckled as though she was his own little smorgasbord of delights that he would take his good time enjoying.

"Not yet." He moved down her stomach and stuck his tongue in her belly button. "Ramon!" she squealed and wiggled. "Stop! That tickles." He laughed and continued licking and kissing her. He spread her legs and looked at her again. "Mi armor, eres hermosa." She felt herself heating at his perusal.

"You are absolutely beautiful. Everywhere. Especially here," he said reverently. He placed a thumb on her clitoris and brushed over it. Then pressed gently through the folds of her labia. "So soft." The dew of her sex accumulated in the deep folds of her tissues and on the tip of her clitoris, which seemed harder and firmer than when he'd begun his perusal. His mouth watered as he took in her smell, her essence. She smelled of citrus and cinnamon. He continued fingering her clitoris and the folds of her sex, rubbing over the soft, sensuous flower. She moaned and wiggled her hips trying to get purchase for a climax. She was close. It was then that he placed his lips on her clitoris and sucked gently at first and then more vigorously. He placed a long finger in her and rolled it up toward the top of her pelvis bone, near where her clitoris was anchored. "Ramon! Don't stop. Yes," she shouted.

The coming climax rose in her groin. As he placed one large hand under her buttocks and sucked her deeply, she felt a tension in her belly and then in her groin. Her legs stiffened and her bottom clenched as she spiraled out of control, her spasm, the strongest orgasm she had ever had. As she came back to earth, she felt him lift her in his arms and carry her to the opposite double bed. He'd pulled back the covers and lay down beside her. She looked at him and brushed a hand down the side of his face. He smiled. Then she realized that they were not finished. She looked down at his burgeoning penis, large and hard.

"Let me return the favor," she said, scooting down the bed.

"No, Beth, I want to be inside you," he said.

"In a minute." She reached for his cock and began rubbing it between her hands. He sucked in a deep breath as she licked it from the base to the tip where a bit of fluid leaked out. The feel of his erect penis excited her. Her breasts felt full. Her excitement was unmanageable. She rubbed his penis between her breasts and then used the tip of one breast to rub against his cock.

"Beth, please, sweetheart," he breathed deeply. "I can't hold on much longer."

She took his cock into her mouth and suckled it, lapping at the head and cupping his balls with her hands. Her warm mouth encircled him, and she took him deep to the back of her throat and then out. She continued to use her hands to milk him, playing with the head of his penis with her mouth. She fondled his balls and sucked sweetly, making smacking noises on the most sensitive part of his anatomy, the head. "Beth," he shouted. The sensations were so sweet, so exciting, he could hold it no longer. When he let go, the gush of semen was so plentiful that some of it dripped out of her mouth, but most of it went down her throat. He heaved, panting and sighing.

47

"Beth, you made me come so hard; come here, mi dulce dama, sweet lady," he said pulling her into his arms. "You're not ever getting away from me."

They lay like that for about an hour when Beth could feel him stirring again. They were lying on their sides with his penis rubbing against her buttocks when he put two fingers on her clitoris and began to rub and press into her, bringing her arousal to a head.

"Can you come for me again, sweet?" he asked. It didn't take her long to have another rousing orgasm. Ramon felt the firm pressure of her "o" ring as she came against his fingers. They kissed then, rolling in one another's arms and dozing for a while. "I will never let you go, sweetheart," he said, looking serious. She winced.

Just then her phone rang. She tensed. He cursed and drew away from her as she rolled off the bed and walked to her purse to get her phone. He enjoyed watching her plump buttocks as she walked.

"I'm sorry, Ramon," she said. "I have to answer this. It could be Gina." He sat up realizing she could be right. He put on his pants and shirt and gathered her clothing.

"When did it happen?" she asked. "I'll be right there."

"What happened?" he asked. "Someone tried to burgle the house," she said. Aunt Maddy interrupted the burglar. The police are there." He said nothing but tensely helped her into her clothes. He checked his gun, and she looked in her purse for hers. They looked into one another's eyes as if they were again in the service, pledged to protect.

5 PROTECTION

When they arrived at the West End house, police cars lit up the neighborhood like holiday lights, and an ambulance was parked in the wide driveway. Beth wondered whether the intruder had hurt Maddy. But as she walked by the ambulance, she saw a man, unconscious and laid out. They were giving him oxygen. Aunt Maddy stood to the side along with Uncle Gerald, who was holding a blanket to Aunt Maddy. She fussed at him.

"I don't need a blanket," she said. "It's too hot for a blanket. Stop that." She swatted at his hands. Just then, Gina came over with a neighbor, Janet, who often played cards with Aunt Maddy.

"Hi, Gina, Aunt Maddy, what happened here?" Beth asked. "Is the man in the ambulance the one who broke in your house, Aunt Maddy?"

"Yes, the young idiot," Maddy said. "He was after these I think," she said, holding out the small travel drives for computers. Gina took them from her and looked around at the police who seemed to be finished taking statements and were preparing to leave.

"Did you say anything about the computer drives?"

Beth asked, looking at Aunt Maddy. Maddy shook her head, "No. I thought that if he considered them important, it might be a better idea to give them to you to see what was so darn special about them. He clearly went through things at Gina's house too because the door over there was open as well."

"Did you notice that, Aunt Maddy? Or did you assume?"

"I noticed it, you ninny. You didn't think I would assume something so important, would you? The sliding glass door to Gina's house was open. That's the first thing I noticed. Then I noticed ours was too. That was too much of a coincidence." Chills went through Beth, and she shivered with the realization that Aunt Maddy and Uncle Gerald as well as Gina could have been seriously hurt. Fortunately, Gina got her message, but didn't think to warn Aunt Maddy and Uncle Gerald. They had a shotgun, but rarely used it. Ramon placed a comforting arm around Beth's shoulders, pulling her near him. He listened quietly as Aunt Maddy told the story again.

She complained about having to tell the police the story, but also having to explain it all again in more precise detail. Midway between her second telling of the story, one of her friends, Alice, walked up to the officers and gave them a list of all of the vehicles that had driven down Sportsman's Road in the last couple of weeks. A police officer walked over on the crunching gravel and approached Beth and Ramon. Ramon bent his head and whispered to Beth that they should tell the police who they were.

"Aunt Maddy, give us a minute," Beth said, interrupting Maddy's recitation, thankfully coming to an end.

Beth and Ramon walked to the police where they showed their identification. "Actually, we're semi-retired, but there are some loose ends that seem to be following us from the service," she explained.

"Can you say more about that, ma'am?" the officer asked.

"No, at this time I can't," said Beth. "I was attacked earlier this evening. The two events could be connected. We're not certain."

"Are you working on apprehending the persons involved?" asked Ramon. Another police person, an attractive dark-skinned woman walked up to them, her radio blaring. He recognized her as someone with whom he had attended school. "Cathy," he said. "Or should I say Officer Elton?" She nodded her head and held out a hand to shake it. They had been friends when he was a teen. They had history. She knew a woman who knew him very well — too well. He grimaced internally and hoped things would not get awkward. It had been a long time since he'd seen or even thought about Barbara. She had taught him the mechanics of sex. Cathy was her niece — a tall, and muscled African American woman who had attended Galveston College to get prepared for the police academy. Some people thought the two of them had a thing going because he was at Barbara's house often when he was younger.

"Good to see you, Ramon," she said. "Long time no see. Sorry we can't be of more help here. We'll check out this list of license plate numbers given to us by your aunt's friend and see what we come up with. Except for the guy who was clocked by your aunt, we didn't see anyone else." Cathy kept her facial expressions impersonal. Maybe she'd forgotten about him and *her* aunt.

Ramon didn't correct Cathy about the relationship between Maddy and himself. Beth gave him a quizzical look and smiled. He squeezed her shoulder and made introductions between the two women.

"We aren't certain who exactly the suspects are and why they're targeting us," Beth said. "However, if they're getting this close to us, they must be desperate." The two officers conferred with another set of officers who decided to leave the scene for another call. One other officer with another car stayed behind, searching the neighborhood for a possible accomplice.

"There's nothing we can do right now as the suspect is still unconscious. We'll charge him with breaking and entering," Cathy said. "We found glass on the deck indicating that he'd broken the door. However, we're not sure how he got into your aunt's and uncle's house."

"I can think of a number of ways that could be done," Beth said. "However, right now, I'm concerned about getting my elderly relatives back into their home and settled down. We would appreciate it if you could send someone to canvass the neighborhood and drive by for a while until we know who this is and have apprehended him. Obviously, whoever it is is working with more than one person." Beth gave information about her attack and why she thought she was the focus of the assault. The details would need to wait. She wasn't certain exactly what the culprits were looking for, but she would find out. For now, it was best to say as little as possible.

Ramon considered an assault on Beth and her family to be an assault on himself. He inspected the property and turned the information over and over in his head before he decided. Beth would need to move in with him. But would she agree to it? This was a dangerous situation. It was obvious someone was after Beth, but why? He needed to get her away from her family and in a safe place where he could protect her. This thing had gone on long enough. It was time to call in reinforcements. His brothers were sure to find this a pleasant change of pace. Since the thugs who had attacked his family's restaurant, they hadn't had much of a challenge. His brothers were as quick as he was and deadly when they had to be. They all lived in the same general area, a quaint, quiet neighborhood in League City.

His mother had insisted that they buy there before League City became a boomtown. Their only other relative in Galveston was a cousin, Carlos, who had retired from the college as a maintenance worker. He owned some modest homes. Carlos offered to sell Ramon two of his homes, as he was tiring of managing too many properties. Before he had quit the service, Ramon had planned ahead, asking for help from his brothers at restoring the houses, and as a result, the Vela brothers and their families always had more than one place to stay in Galveston. It was to one of these neighborhood homes that he planned to invite Beth.

The trick was to get Beth to move in with him. That was going to be a challenge. She wouldn't want to leave her family unprotected. So he would need to think ahead of her there. He helped her family back into their home, helped clean up and checked to be certain some fingerprints had been taken. He covered up the holes in the glass doors at both Gina's place and at Maddy and Gerald's. They would call a glass repair company in the morning for the sliding glass doors. Ramon got on his phone to ask his brother Mateo if he would mind helping to guard the family. When Mateo arrived, Ramon made introductions to Gina, Maddy and Gerald, who were all gathered in Gina's lounge area. Gina offered Mateo a guest room some distance from her room and Beth's.

Mateo was of average height, with black hair and brown eyes. A muscled and lean young man in his early 30s, he appeared to be as fit as his brother, but with a quiet disposition. Mateo had wanted to be a priest in his younger years, but was sidetracked when he stopped his studies to help a friend on drugs. His eyes glinted as he gave a brief perusal to Gina. It was obvious that Mateo was a proud man, protective and loyal to his family. But it did not go unnoticed by everyone that he was interested in Gina. As Gina showed Mateo his room, Ramon escorted Maddy and

Gerald to their home and returned to the lounge area. Beth sat on the loveseat with her hands over her face. Her long brown hair shone in the dim light of the sitting room. He walked to her and sat down, pulling her close to his side.

"Beth, you and I know that this has gone beyond serious," he said, looking down at her. "Someone is desperate to get something you have. What do you think it is?"

"I don't know," she said, blowing out air and leaning back on the sofa. "I've been wracking my brains trying to think what these asses might be searching for, but. . ." She frowned and dug the travel drives out of the pocket of her caftan. "Do you think the McKeans had something stored on these drives or on one of their computers that someone wants?"

"It could be, Beth," he said. "But most people engaged in finding something like this are likely to do their snooping in your computer, without ever entering your home. Whatever they are searching for must not be on your computer. Did you store something from the McKeans' computer before you left?"

She frowned thinking back to what she did before leaving their home. "They had sufficient cyber security to prevent theft," she said. "I turned over all of their equipment to the agency before I left. However, I did copy some files that I thought might be useful in helping Val to find them."

"What did you copy them to?" he asked. She looked around and placed a finger over her lips. She walked to her room and dug out a signal detector. When she returned to Gina's sitting area, she used the device to check the room for listening devices. Nothing seemed to be turning up. To be on the safe side, she beckoned him outdoors to the deck, giving the same sweep to that area. When she was satisfied, she spoke to him in a near whisper.

"I copied the stuff to some travel drives," she said. "I

hid them well before I left Gina's house."

"Are these the drives?" he asked pointing to the ones in her hand.

"No, I have them in a place that might be difficult for someone to locate." Beth could see Ramon's shoulders relax.

"Beth, I want to propose something," he said. She tensed as she heard the word "propose."

"It's not that kind of proposal," he said smiling. "Though someday I would like to . . . Well, right now, let's take it one step at a time. Would you consider moving in with me? I have a house in town, mid Galveston. We own some houses in a quiet neighborhood. One of the rooms in my house is set up for preventing the kind of snooping that we know is common. And, my other brothers and some cousins would be there to be certain that we are safe."

"I don't know, Ramon," she said. "What about my own family? I appreciate your asking Mateo to be here for my family, but I feel somehow that I'm the one who should be protecting them."

"I understand your concerns," he said. "However, whoever is attacking you is after what you have on those travel drives. I would bet that's what they are after. We need time to investigate each one and to analyze what's there. That's going to take time and a secure area. So, if you remove yourself and your belongings to my house, it's likely whoever is after what you have will follow you there. That would be the best way to keep you and your family safe."

6 MOVING IN

It didn't take Beth long to pack her belongings and go with him to the home he had bought in a quiet neighborhood well behind the seawall and some distance from the busy tourist district. The tree-covered street was tucked away in the 3800 block of Avenue P½. Ramon took her bag out of the trunk and led her, placing a protective hand in the small of her back, up the few steps and into the two-story house. The oak tree on the front lawn seemed to hide the house from the view of the outside world.

When his parents had written to him asking whether he wanted to invest in the neighborhood, he had hesitated. The island had its share of storms, and buying on the island had to be done with consideration. After some research, he found that the house itself, sitting higher than usual on the block, was safe from rising tides and that the water rarely, if ever, reached the neighborhood. Most of the homes sat a few more feet above what was necessary. His brothers and cousins had helped him with renovations — adding new bathrooms, expanding the kitchen and adding a pool to the back yard. When he walked in the door, a young man greeted them from the top of the narrow steps to the right of door. Beth could smell the aroma of sandalwood wafting around the man as he came to a halt in front of them.

"Alejandro," Ramon said, making introductions. "This is Beth Larsen," he said smiling at her possessively. He sensed the surprise in Beth as she looked at Alejandro. Most women found him extremely attractive; in addition, the two men were almost identical in appearance. Alejandro was not one to be shy about the women who were drawn to him. He came down the last step and picked up her hand and kissed it. Beth blushed and looked at Ramon.

"Does he do this all the time?" she asked.

"Yes, but this time, you'd better keep your distance," Ramon said, glaring at his brother. Alejandro laughed.

"Ah, little brother," he said, with a slight accent. "You have nothing to worry about if you are keeping this sweet chica happy," he said. Ramon blew out air and clipped his brother on the shoulder.

"That's enough," he said. "Beth is going to need your help. We think someone is trying to kill her and is looking for something she might have."

Alejandro's demeanor changed immediately. He was all business, standing stiffly and tall. He took Beth's bag from his brother and turned to tell him in Spanish to show her around.

As Ramon showed her around the spacious house, she relaxed. There was a sense of quiet and protectiveness about the place and about the two brothers. Ramon showed her a secret cabinet for weapons and another one upstairs. He showed her to her room, which had a connecting door to his bedroom.

"I get my own room," she said, with a bit of sarcasm, and sat down on the bed.

"Of course," Ramon said, not missing her intended dig but not responding directly to it. "We have plenty of rooms here." He sat down beside her. He wanted to pick up where they left off at the hotel, but he couldn't bring himself to do so. It was close to dawn and they were both exhausted.

"Oh, I forgot to show you this too," he stood and walked to another door that stood between the two rooms. It opened up into a luxurious bathroom with a Jacuzzi tub and shower. "If you feel like having a bath before resting, I'll turn on the water in the tub."

"That would be nice," she said. He prepared the water, while Beth put up her clothing in the dresser drawers in her bedroom. The bed was covered with a grey duvet and four or five plump silver and blue pillows. Light colored furniture was placed around the room, giving it a modern Swedish look. A large lamp was on the bed stand. By the time she was finished putting up her things, the bath was ready and smelled fragrant, like lavender.

"Your bath awaits you, mi reina, my queen," Ramon said, with a slight bow. She smiled. He had gone into his own room to change into a robe. When he came back to her room to announce her bath, he looked as though he wanted to ravish her. But he knew that she was tired. He helped her get her clothes off and led her to the tub. Her smooth olive skin was enticing and brown hair hung down her back. His cock grew hard when he saw her sit down in the warm fragrant water. "May I join you?"

She looked up at him. "I don't think I'm any good to you, Ramon," she said. "I'm so tired. I think I'll probably fall asleep right here in the tub."

"The better reason for me to get in with you to make certain you do not drown," he said, smiling at her and taking off his robe. As he removed the garment, she sucked in air at the beauty of his body. He was all sleek muscle and smooth brown skin. His penis jutted out, hard and ready. She licked her lips. As he got in the other end of the tub, she reached out and stroked his cock.

"If you do that, we will never get out of this tub," he said.

"I know, but you look like you need help," she said.

"I do, but let's get you cleaned up and into bed first."
He took a washcloth and soaped it and washed her arms.
He paid careful attention to her breasts and smoothed the
cloth across her belly. Beth's nipples hardened. She gasped
as he ran the washcloth gently between her legs. As he
massaged her shoulders and brought her between his legs,
he wondered whether he could convince her to take their
relationship seriously. There was so much distance between
them now.

There were problems to solve. The first priority was
getting her clear of this threat to her life. Maybe they were
thinking of it the wrong way. Perhaps it would be best for
him to contact those within the agency to allow them to
help with the problem. It wasn't unheard of for agents or
former agents to be targeted for some reason, but with all
the budget cuts in the departments now, it became more
difficult to find someone to help with what many inside the
division would consider a minor problem. He sighed as he
thought about the complications that awaited them
tomorrow. But it would not do to let her think that those
problems were insurmountable.

He had to have hope. While he no longer participated
in his mother's religion, he considered it a good lesson in
having confidence that things would work out in the end. It
was that attitude that was necessary as the two of them
faced the difficulties that lay ahead. Her head leaned back
on his chest and he could tell that she was falling asleep.
"Come on, sleepy head," he said, standing and pulling her
to him. "It's time to get you in bed."

He wrapped the large towel around her, stepped out of
the tub and lifted her to him in his arms. He walked her to
the bed and dried her, pulled the covers back and laid her
down. Her eyes were already closed, her head lolling about.
He kissed her on the forehead and covered her to her chin,
turned off the lamp beside her bed and looked down on
her. She was beautiful; in her relaxed state, she looked like

more child than woman. He couldn't believe his luck in finding her. She was perfect for him. Now, if he could only convince her that they were meant to be together.

7 TO COMMIT OR NOT

Beth felt a warm body wrapped around hers. The feeling of being totally safe and cocooned in firm comfort seeped into her bones. The unmistakable firm erection nestled against her buttocks. She sighed and kept her eyes closed. She needed to make a decision. There was no mistaking the need in Ramon. But could she answer that need? It had been years since she had had a lasting love affair. It had been so long ago. The first time she'd made love with a man, it was painful and distasteful. She was certain that she'd never want a man to try plowing between her thighs. The man who had convinced her to let him was quick and selfish. She'd been in her 20s. It was after a date with one of her colleagues. They had been drinking. He was clearly intent on having her.

In the confusion of the moment, he had spent little time preparing her. After he had forced himself inside her, she decided that would be the last time she would allow herself to lose control of a situation. They were both young. But he was more than old enough to know better. However, she let him know in no uncertain terms that it would not happen again.

There was only one other lover after him. He was in a committed relationship with another woman and told her only after they had been together once. That was enough to make her determined never to do it again. So she turned her back on dating, sex, love, or the chance for it. It was easy to pour herself into her work from then on. Now and then, her body reminded her that her biological clock was ticking away. She wondered whether having children would be in her future. It didn't seem that way. She'd spent her life being the stand-in mother for the McKeans, but she really didn't feel the time slipping away, until it was obvious that the family had disintegrated.

Now, Ramon was pressing her to commit to a relationship, to having sex, regularly. They had good foreplay, but no real consummation. Perhaps if she could keep him from the final act, they could back away from one another. It seemed that love and satisfying sex were not in the cards for her. She had given up on it. Just then, Ramon stirred and placed a hand on her arm. He pressed into her backside, rubbing against her. He got out of bed and went to the restroom. She lay on her side pretending to be asleep. She felt the bed dip as he entered again and put his arms around her. "I know you're awake, my sweet," he whispered. She turned to look at him. He pulled hair out of her eyes.

"You were a sleepy duck," he said, smiling.

"Yes, I was," she yawned, covering her mouth. She smiled and got out of bed, going to the restroom to brush her teeth. "Can I use this toothbrush?" she asked at the door of the bathroom. "Of course," he said.

When she arrived back at the bed, she debated whether she wanted to get back in it. The mild fall weather made it chilly in the house. He looked up at her, the evidence of his erection tenting the covers. "Come back to bed, mi amor," he said. "The day is escaping us."

"Ramon, I don't know whether I want to go this far,"

she said taking a small step back. She realized that going this far with him might create a level of commitment that she was not ready to embrace.

"What are you afraid of, my sweet? That you will fall madly in love with me and not be able to turn back?" He smiled and grabbed her hand tugging her back into the bed and on top of him. She felt the power of his arms as he lifted her to straddle him. A thin robe she had grabbed in the bathroom fell open under his questing fingers. He embraced her under the robe, smoothing a hand down her back and across her buttocks.

"Yes," she said, as long dormant feelings began to stir in her. "That's exactly what I'm afraid of. I don't want to get. . . " Before she could finish the sentence, Ramon ducked his head under her and enclosed the nipple of her breast in his mouth and suckled. The answering contractions in her center awakened her sexuality. This was the first time in a long time that she would go this far having sex. Her body seemed to be saying that what she had experienced in the past was nothing.

She was lost in him, and it frightened her. There was no turning back now. He flipped her over on her back and kissed down her stomach, to the thatch of curls at her core. His tongue found her clitoris and flicked across it, sometimes pushing against it, sometimes, rolling it between his lips. "Ohhh, Ramon. Yes." The moisture coming from her pussy was undeniable. She thought back to times when she had had sex earlier in her life. It had been nothing like this. She was becoming eager. She wanted to be filled. Ramon came back up to her mouth, kissing her deeply. She could taste herself on his lips. He used a knee to part her legs. She felt his large cock nestled at her entrance. He moved his penis gently across the lips of her labia, around and around the outside of her plump swollen lips. He teased her with the head of his rod, pushing in a bit and pulling out.

"Ramon! Please, please," she said.

"You want this, sweet?" He pushed in her a little more and withdrew.

"Tell me you want it. Tell me you want me." She groaned and wrapped her arms around him.

"Yes, I want you, Ramon. I want you. Please." He sank into her slowly, the head of his large, hard cock stretching her. It felt as though he wouldn't fit.

"It won't," she said, breathlessly.

"Yes, it will," he said chuckling. "How long has it been, sweet?"

"A long time." He rested above her on his elbows, holding still as he pressed a little further inside her, finally settling deeply inside and staying quite still.

"Are you OK?" he asked. "I don't want to hurt you if you can't." His voiced sounded strained as though he were trying to hold himself back.

"Ramon, if you stop, I will scream," she said.

"You will scream my love, but not with frustration," he said, moving out and then back into her. He began quick short movements and remained still. Then moved again. Finally, he moved steadily inside her, in out. She could not remember ever feeing so loved, so well treated in bed. He was tender but firm, holding her gently, touching her reverently and kissing her as he plunged inside her. The feeling of being encompassed within his love was unmistakable. As he quickened his movements, she felt the unmistakable contraction of a climax, something she had not experienced in so long, that for the first time in a long time, she knew this was what she wanted.

"Ramooon!" She keened. He chuckled, and then made a choking sound deep in his throat as his own release hit him, spewing powerfully inside her, so strong that he could not contain his joy. He continued to rock into her, slowing gradually, panting. As he withdrew from her, he pulled her on top of him.

He smoothed her hair from her face and kissed her, then rolled her to the side and spooned with her, wrapping his arms around her. "Beth, you are amazing." Her tight, wet pussy had milked him dry. He could not remember ever having this kind of experience. While his first woman was much older than him and had taught him all he knew about making love, the depth of his emotions combined with the strong physical attraction to Beth made him feel forever bound to her. There was no way he would let her go.

His deep voice rumbled through her, arousing her again. "Beth, sweetheart. Are you OK?" he whispered. She nodded and rolled over to face him. She lay there stunned at the enormity of what they had experienced, unable to speak. He had been so attentive, so loving; she was overwhelmed. Her brown eyes glittered with unshed tears as she grappled with the impact of loving this man.

Now, she knew what it was like to be loved, truly loved. And with that realization, her heart opened. Beth realized that everything she had been taught about her place in life, about the kind of man she should be with, had changed. This man had made her see, no understand, in a way that she had never understood before. The sex she had had in her early life was painful and uninspiring. This was incredible. It wasn't just sex though. It was his statement to her. He had had to show her what he meant. And he did, emphatically. There would be no turning back now. She knew that this man captivated her. The incongruity of it came to her as she struggled to stay awake. He was younger than her and knew more than her about not only making love but also loving. How could that be? It was too much. They both fell fast asleep in one another's arms.

8 MAMA MATCHMAKING

Francisca Maria Garcia Vela considered her growing brood of grandchildren to be the highlight of her life. It didn't matter that she had helped her husband build a family business into a chain of Mexican food restaurants. The family had done it together. They had begun with one restaurant when their children were young, and now, their assets and their holdings were diverse. They had branched out in the Houston area and were now prepared for retirement. The children were managing the restaurants that they had decided to keep. Now, her only task was to be certain all of her children were happily married. Her two daughters, Rosa and Isabella, had men in their lives. Isabella had been her best helper over the years. The truth of the matter was that had it not been for Isabella's brilliant financial guidance, the family business would never have grown as it did.

Francisca was always awestruck at how deft her daughter was at not only being a secondary manager, and a good one, but at being the older sibling who watched her younger sister and brothers. Isabella was dating a man who would certainly marry her. They set the date earlier this year;

it would be a wedding to remember. Francisca recalled her simple wedding in San Antonio. She and Nicolas had not two nickels to rub together. But they were in love and it was because of that love that she and Nicolas worked so hard. It was Francisca's boss who told her of the restaurant opportunity. A family friend had led to another family member who they didn't know they had in the Houston area. Soon, they were doing better and the hand-to-mouth life was behind them.

Rosa was happy too. She had married Walter Belmount, son of an old Houston family that lived in the River Oaks district. His parents objected to Rosa at first. But Walter was their only child and when they saw that the two could not live without one another, they quickly acquiesced. Rosa and Walter now had two children and were living in the same neighborhood as his parents.

The boys were a different issue altogether. Nicolas Jr. insisted on taking the reins of the family business along with Isabella. Now that it appeared that things were well underway with the two other locations they had opened in Sugarland and Tomball, Nicolas was sure to select a wife from the many women who dated him. Mateo was a different matter. The boy was reluctant to be around people period. Extremely shy, he wanted to join the priesthood, but had become mixed up with that no-good friend who was hooked on drugs. Francisca had tried to tell Mateo not to associate with Toni, but Mateo was determined to see his friend use his life for good. He was constantly out with Toni, making certain he got into no trouble.

Alejandro had found a sweet girl and married her early. Sarah had fit right into the family. There was no doubt that they would be together. The woman was simply crazy about her son. Alejandro was most protective of family. When the criminals were preying on their business, Alejandro somehow made all the problems go away. He never said what he did. She was careful not to ask. Nicolas was

67

disappointed that he was unable to help his son with the problem, but apparently the people responsible for the issues were young people Alejandro knew. Now, he was settled with his family, and they were expecting another child.

But, her youngest son, Ramon, was finally home from serving in some secret government organization, and she wanted him to help with the family business. Ramon could cook, but that's not what they needed him to do. They had cooks, managers, waiters and waitresses. They paid a good wage and even found a way to help their employees set up retirement accounts. But what they needed was someone to make the rounds to be certain that quality was good at all of the restaurants. Ramon needed to get married, to settle down. Francisca looked in her walk-in closet to select a dress for the day. Everything was organized in neat cubicles. The closet was more like a small room. She looked at herself in the mirror; she'd put on weight over the years. Ah well, having six children would do that to a woman. Still, she thought, sucking in her gut, she was a good-looking woman. She sat at the dresser where she put on her makeup and brushed her hair.

It would be perfect if she could get Ramon interested in Sarah's sister, Jessica. The girl was beautiful; Ramon would not be able to resist her. Jessica was always coming to the restaurant near Rice University to keep her sister company. Sarah helped make certain the orders were getting to customers as they should and helped oversee the kitchens. Occasionally, she cooked when there was an emergency. She had mentioned that Ramon was home and Jessica looked hopeful, excited even. She had to be careful not to push too hard. But, maybe that was what was needed first, just a little push in the right direction. She smiled in the mirror. Things would work out fine.

When she arrived at the restaurant, Vela's, everyone was doing what they did best, serving the best food and making the environment pleasant for customers. Ramon sat in the back drinking a glass of wine and sampling the tapas. She rushed to his table and gave him a hug. "It's about time, mi hijo," she said, tearing up. "What took you so long to come home?"

"I was just here last fall, Mama," he said. "You look good. How have you been feeling?" She sat down in the booth opposite to him.

"Oh, I have been doing fine. Just a few little aches and pains, nothing serious. Were you able to get all the things finished for your work? Are you going to be home for good now?"

"Yes, Mama. It's likely I will help Nicolas run the restaurants," he said.

She beamed. "I am so happy to hear that. Your brother works so hard. It would be nice for him to have someone to help so that he can take a vacation."
They sat for a while listening to the music, and a waiter brought his mother lemonade and another plate so she could share the tapas. She waved at a friend across the room. "That's Alva Rider," she said. "We need to talk about the parish project that is coming up. We're helping with a food drive for the homeless. Would you like to join us, Ramon?"

"No, Mama, not yet," he said. "I have some problems to work out." He fiddled with his napkin as though he had something more to say, but did not know how to say it.

"You know your brother's wife has a sister who works in the restaurant sometimes. There she is over there." She waved at Jessica. A tall pretty blond woman came over to speak to his mother. Ramon had his back to the restaurant door and couldn't see her until she arrived at the table. She smiled at him and gave him that kind of appraisal that women did when they were wondering whether a man was free. He looked away to give her the hint that he was not. But she slipped into the booth beside him anyway.

"Hello, Ramon," she said, holding out a hand to shake his. She licked her lips and pushed her considerable bosom out. "I've heard so much about you."

"Really," he said, glancing at his mother. "I hope it was good."

"Of course," she said, giggling. She flipped her hair; it flicked in his face. She squirmed in her seat. Just then, Francisca got up from her seat, muttering that she had to see a friend. She gave them a tight smile, smoothed her dress down and walked away.

Everything seemed to be moving in slow motion. Ramon was anxious to leave too, but the woman would not move. He wanted to ask her politely to allow him to leave, but he couldn't think of a way to do it without seeming crass. He knew, of course, what his mother was up to. There wasn't a time that he'd visited that she had not tried throwing some woman at him. She just did not understand him. She once asked one of his brothers if he was gay. Alejandro laughed, "Ramon? Surely you are joking, Madre." He only called her mother when he was serious. Only Alejandro knew of the torrid affair Ramon had had with the older woman, Barbara, who had taught Ramon how to be with a woman. Not just to make love, but how to be with her. That was an art. Ramon rubbed a hand over his face in an effort to quell the emotions that threatened to rip from him. Jessica continued a one-sided conversation with herself.

"My friend Heather is planning her wedding, and we have just picked out her dress. She's dressing in mostly pure white but she's got all this pink that she wants included with the trim and the other stuff that goes with the dress. You should see it," she went on and on. Ramon looked past her to the bar and motioned to his sister Rosa, who was helping. She took one look at Ramon and Jessica and realized immediately what the problem was. She walked over with lemonade in her hand. She placed it on the table.

"Hi, Jessica. Nicolas was wondering if you could help with a problem he has at the back," she said.

"Oh," Jessica's face fell. "We were just having such a great conversation. We were getting to know one another. I was just about to. ..."

"Yes, I know," Rosa said, keeping her deadpan poker face on. "But you see, I think this problem is only one that you can help Nicolas with." She said it more pointedly, motioning to the back door of the restaurant. Jessica frowned and looked at Ramon.

"Well, if you don't think you'll mind, Ramon," she said as though she were out of breath. Jessica put him in mind of Marilyn Monroe. He wondered if she spent her spare time watching old reruns of Monroe and practicing the pout of her lips and the thrust of her breasts. He was certain that there was not a cogent thought in her mind. Jessica rose from the padded booth and turned to look at him.

"I hope we can spend more time together," she said, looking hopefully.

"I can't say," Ramon said, not wanting to make a date with her, but not wanting to hurt her feelings, since she was, after all, family in a way. "I have . . ."

"What he means to say, Jessica, is that he just arrived home and has many things to do before he can think of dating," Rosa blurted out for him. She placed a reassuring hand on Jessica's shoulder and whispered in her ear. That made Jessica grin and she turned, waved coyly at Ramon and nearly skipped away.

"What did you say to her?" Ramon asked.

"I'm not answering any questions until I get my hug from my little brother," she said. He stood and gave her a bear hug and kiss on the cheek. Rosa was short and slim where he was tall and muscled. Often people wondered whether they were from the same family. Rosa slid in the booth opposite him. Music from the band began, making it harder to hear. The red leather of the booth couch made for a cozy place to talk. The glistening bottles of liquor on the shelves of the bar and the blur of movement from the barrista as well as the kitchen comforted them both. Waiters scurried around serving customers, putting plates on tables and bringing drinks. The smooth concrete floor was polished to a shine. The image of a matador and bull sat above the bar.

"Thanks, Rosa," he said. "I didn't want to hurt her feelings, but I really am not available." Rosa drank from her glass of lemonade.

"So, you're finally home," she said. "Are you here for good or going back after a break?"

"No, I decided to stop working for the government and start working for the family. I know Mama and Papa want me to help with the business, and it's just as well for me. I grew tired of the operations."

"Yeah, really. That's hard to believe," Rosa said. "You?" Rosa's dark hair fell in waves about her face. "I think there's more to this than you say."

"There is somebody in my life, Rosa," he said slowly, testing her reaction.

"And?"

"And she might not be someone that Mama will approve of," he said, looking in her eyes to further gage her reaction.

"This is the woman you talked about last Christmas? Or was it Christmas before last?" she asked.

"Her name is Beth," he said. "And I need your help, Rosa." She frowned.

"Wait a minute. This is serious," she said, taking another gulp of her lemonade. "Why do you need my help?"

"She is older than me," he said; several seconds passed. He looked at the band and then looked at her. "Much older than me." Rosa took a deep breath and reached a hand over to her brother and squeezed it.

"Do you love her?"

"So much it hurts," he said. "She doesn't think we should be together and thinks the difference in our age will be an impediment to our relationship. I can't convince her otherwise. And then there's the fact that Mama is going to object and probably throw stumbling blocks in our way."

"Give me a chance to work on her, Ramon," she said. "Mama only wants you to be happy. When she realizes that Beth makes you happy, she will do what's best for you."

"I hope you're right," he said. "But this can't be something that she has any experience with at all. Something that is totally foreign to her. She wants to fill the house with more grandchildren. I don't think Beth wants that. At least, I'm not sure about it."

"Ramon, don't think of that. Remember some important things here. First, it's loving each other that is important. If this is your great love, it would be foolish to back away because your mother does not agree. Second, if Beth is worth it, she will realize that age is not a factor. Third, women have children late in life all the time; if she is willing, it can be done. And also, we have plenty of grandchildren in this family already, to say nothing of the ones Mama knows nothing about." Ramon's eyebrows shot up.

"You mean, Nicolas? Uhh. You mean he has."

"Let's not talk about that. We need to get to work at smoothing things over with Mama. I want you to start by sending me some pictures of you and Beth. We're going to have a family party in a couple of weeks; it's going to be an engagement party for Isabella. Bring her then. In the meantime, let me work on Mama and drum up some support for you."

He squeezed Rosa's hand across the table. "Thanks, Rosa, you're the best." She scooted over to the edge of the booth and stood, walked the step to where Ramon sat and pulled his head down so she could kiss him on the forehead. She patted him on the shoulder for good measure and walked back to the bar. Ramon stared at the glass in front of him thinking of the delicious time he had spent with Beth before coming to his family's restaurant. She was so surprised at the satisfaction she experienced that she nearly cried. He wondered what an uncaring bastard had done to her to make her so wary of making love to men and how she had come to the grudging acceptance that there was no satisfaction to be had in an intimate relationship.

Her curves and soft breasts were enough to inspire any man to lasting devotion. He thought of the moment he had breached her, for she was so tight that he was sure that she had not made love in quite some time. He had to be careful not to hurt her. Before he'd penetrated her, she was so wet and ready for him, that he had little trouble getting in, but he had had to take it slow. She was so delicate, so sweet.

He couldn't wait to get back to her so they could make love again. It wasn't just the love making that made things special between them; it was the things he could talk about with Beth that Jessica would never have the ability or interest to consider. There was their long history of working together —their understanding of a different world in law enforcement that not even the police generally understood. There was also her keen intelligence; he knew from her records that her intelligence scores were high. That didn't mean that everyone who topped out on the intelligence scale was easy to talk to or had something to say. Then, there were those times in Connecticut when they relaxed together, cooking and enjoying his latest rose grafts.

That was what made Beth different; she was intelligent without trying. She had that something about her that made her fun to be with and interesting to talk to. She appreciated his interests. She understood things without his having to explain because they'd worked together and because they simply shared a core set of values that made solving problems together engaging. The most important part of his esteem for Beth was that he loved her. He wondered whether she would ever love him as he did her. He was willing to gamble on it. Surely she could feel what he felt for her. Surely. At some point, he had to convince her that this wasn't just recreational sex.

However, there was the problem of the parties trying to kill her and to get something that she might have. He'd left her and his brother working at her computer in the small, high-security study at the house. It was time to return to see whether they had discovered anything of value. He walked out of his family's restaurant and took a stroll through Rice Village to get to his car. On the way, he stopped at a jewelry store and stared at the rings in the window.

9 PROBLEMS

Alejandro had met many women in his time, but Beth was one who befuddled him. She sat at her laptop working in a language few understood. Her fingers raced across the keyboard. His brother, Ramon, had asked him to look after her while he went to visit with family. Ramon had an interesting set of circumstances before him. There was no doubt that Beth would fit into their family, but convincing their mother that Beth was right for Ramon might be a bit of a challenge. Mama was apt to meddle in the affairs of her children.

Sometimes, he wondered whether success was such a good thing. When his mother had to work all the time, she was too tired to meddle much. In fact, he remembered getting away with quite a lot while his parents and his older siblings struggled to make the family business a success. But it wasn't long before that happened, and then Mama had too much time on her hands. Once the last baby, Ramon, was born, she was free to do more with her life. She volunteered for social service projects in Houston and League City and was active in her parish church.

But that was not going to be an insurmountable

problem for Ramon. He could tell that the biggest problem would be Beth herself. She was unassuming and quiet. Her pretty brown eyes and rich brown hair were warmly inviting. Were it not for his wife, Sarah, he could be jealous of his little brother. How had he found such a beauty? And so intelligent, resourceful and independent too. At about 5 feet 8 inches, she seemed more petite, slender. But she had a certain amount of tinsel strength to her. She wore a long blue flowered tunic over dark jeans, her long hair pulled back from her face in a ponytail. "Any luck?" he asked, standing over her shoulder and peering at the screen as she worked.

"Not yet," she said, shaking her head. Her fingers continued to race across the keyboard. He left the study to get coffee. That morning, before Ramon left for Houston, Alejandro had made them breakfast. She'd appreciated the comfortable verbal sparring he and his brother frequently enjoyed with one another. He observed the intense expressions his brother, Ramon, flicked in her direction. He didn't want Alejandro to notice, but he did. Alejandro knew this wasn't just any attraction. His brother had fallen, hard. He wondered how Ramon planned to include Beth in his life now that he was resigning from the service.

It would take some adjustments for her. He had no doubt that the men in his family would embrace her. His two sisters and his wife certainly would, with time. His mother, that was a different story altogether. She was steeped in religious conservatism and would not look kindly on Ramon stepping outside the boundaries she perceived to be appropriate for a young man. Ramon might as well have told his mother he was gay. Well, that might be difficult. His mother had deep-seated prejudices and might fight to bend him to her will.

But time would tell. His mother would need to come to terms with her changing family when the time came. Would she have a big enough heart to embrace them all?

Would she turn away her own son because he did not agree with her on some things? Alejandro could not see his mother bending her will; she was strongly opinionated and made no secret of her views. But she did love her family above all things. For that, he admired her. He had turned to look out the kitchen window when he noticed the couple rubbing their feet against one another. He turned back to see them absorbed in silent communication again, looking at one another, but trying hard not to say anything that might offend Alejandro.

"So, my brother tells me that you two worked together for some time," he said, more as a statement than a question.

"Yes," she said. "We met on assignment and worked in the same area for a while. Ramon was given other assignments along the way, so we saw each other on and off for quite some time."

"And you've been dating for all this time?" Alejandro asked incredulously. If they had, his brother was better at keeping secrets than he thought.

"Oh no," Ramon said, coming to her defense. "I only just began dating her. I couldn't convince her to consider me seriously."

"Were you otherwise engaged, Ms. Larsen?" Alejandro asked. There was a moment of tense silence as she looked into Alejandro's brown eyes to see whether he was serious. She composed herself before answering.

"I'm not certain what you mean exactly by 'engaged,'" she said. "If you mean whether I had other boyfriends, no. There was no one else."

"No husband. No boyfriends. I find that unusual considering your obvious beauty, Ms. Larsen," Alejandro said, smiling and looking at her as though she were available.

She coughed quietly and cleared her throat. "Call me Beth, please. And, no. There was no one in my life, no amorous connection if that's what you mean. I was busy working." She said it so matter-of-factly that Alejandro's lips curved up in a quick smile. It was a dismissal, an unspoken request to butt out of her personal business.

"I think I might have met you sometime ago at a party," he said, unaffected by her attempt to put distance between them. "It was out at the West End."

"You must have met my twin sister," she said. "We look alike."

"Ah," he said. "That explains all. What a blessing that we have two beauties of your station and intelligence. Is it possible that I might meet your sister some time in the future?" It was apparent that she was not accustomed to this much attention. She blushed and looked down at her plate.

"It's likely," Ramon said. "But I think you should mind your own business for the time being, brother. Ms. Larsen is not available, nor is her sister."

"Well, I think that clears things up," Alejandro said. "When is the wedding?"

Ramon balled up his napkin and threw it at his brother. The two burst out laughing. However, Beth seemed not to see anything humorous in this question. She cleared her throat and finished her food, took a quick swallow of her orange juice and cleared the table of her dishes.

"Sorry, Beth," Alejandro said. "We kid each other all the time in this family."

She wouldn't look him in the eye. He looked at his brother and shrugged his shoulders. Ramon shook his head a bit, letting Alejandro know that she was not ready. Alejandro cleared his throat.

"So I understand you're here for some protection," he said. "You've come to the right place. There's no safer place than with the Vela brothers. Just what should we expect?"

Ramon placed his plate in the sink with Beth's and

turned to face his brother. Beth stood on the other side of the table looking at the two brothers.

"The truth is that Beth can mostly take care of herself," Ramon said. "However, it always helps to have another person around just in case. I know you have a gun of your own, Alejandro, and some other weapons. You might want to be certain they are clean and loaded. I need to go see the family to talk to Nicolas and to get more support. Meanwhile, Beth needs to work on finding out what this person wants."

Beth explained that they did not know how many attackers were involved and that she needed someone to keep an eye out for intruders while she explored her hard drive and other equipment. She explained the attack near The Strand in downtown Galveston and also at her family's home.

"Sounds serious," Alejandro said, frowning. "But nothing we can't handle. I have some," he paused, "friends who can help." Ramon had known for some time that his brother had friends among some of the shadier element. His brother had gone into business with a friend who owned a security business. They had ways of contracting workers who could help with testy problems. But he didn't know to what extent his brother could help.

"Leave it to me," Alejandro said. "You'll be able to work undisturbed. Meanwhile, we'll be looking for this perpetrator. Don't worry, little brother. We got your back."

That was hours ago. Since then, Beth had secluded herself in the little study to examine the many files on her devices. Alejandro called his security friends and organized a little team of observers. They spread through the neighborhood at Avenue P½ as well as in her sister's West End neighborhood. There were some suspicious characters in both areas, but no need for concern at this point. He let his friends Jono and Diego watch the area while he checked the perimeter of the house constantly and checked on Beth.

When he arrived for his next 10-minute check, he looked out the window leading to the study and noticed some movement. He called Jono to be sure everything was good. Jono assured him they had noticed nothing unusual, that it was probably one of his guards.

Beth focused on examining each of the several hundred folders that she thought might be the issue. Hidden code could be buried in many ways. She wasn't certain where to begin, but she was sure it would take her some time to find out. She used a couple of programs to help her analyze what could be hidden codes. She realized soon into her search that she would need to let the security agency know that she might be in possession of sensitive information that might have caused the attacks on her life. It would have to be done in a particular way. She had been working for hours when she noticed a ping from Zah, her friend whose computer expertise put her beyond the reach of most techies.

Zah: Hey, I see you've been looking for me.

Beth: Yep, have a problem. Someone's trying to kill me.

Zah: Not good. Why?

Beth: I took some files that my former employers were using. They looked benign, but maybe not.

Zah: Making any progress?

Beth: Some, but I could use your help.

Zah: Give me control.

Beth knew what to do. She trusted Zah to help her go through the folders and to keep the problem under control. Zah had worked for the agency in the past and had many connections that Beth did not. They had done this before and she realized that getting help would be the only way to solve this problem without getting hurt. Beth allowed Zah to work her magic and turned to thank Alejandro for another cup of coffee. She got up from the desk and stretched as Zah worked. After a little more than 30 minutes, Zah pinged her.

Zah: I think I know the problem you're having. Would these "employers" by any chance be involved in apprehending terrorists?

Beth: Likely, but don't know the details.

Zah: I'm going to need to let a contractor know what we're dealing with so you can have some immunity and we can work on solving this problem. I'll let them know that you are in the dark regarding what exactly you're looking for.

Beth: That helps. Any chance they might be able to help with any cleanup if there might be a need or any protection?

Zah: I'll see what I can do.

Zah's avatar image disappeared from the screen, and Beth continued working. About two hours later, Zah marked two folders with some unusual coding that was not apparent upon first observation. When Beth examined the coding a little more carefully, she realized that Zah's hint about the McKeans' work was correct. They apparently had been working to bring down terrorists who had been involved in the World Trade Center bombing. Though that had been years ago, the military and various undercover operations were still working to track down all involved, even peripherally. If they had been successful, they would have worked in Pakistan for a while. She wondered if there was any chance they survived. She was about to shut it down when Ramon placed his hands on her breasts. She leaned her head back as he bent over to kiss her.

"Any luck?" he asked.

"Yes, as a matter of fact, Zah has been helping me," she said. "You remember her?" He nodded.

"Has she found the possible problem?"

"She thinks there are two folders here with some coding in them. It's possible it was used to trace terrorists or to infect their software. We'll know more later. She's also trying to get some protection for me. It seems that this information was sensitive enough to cause a security violation. So, we'll need her help."

She stood up and stepped into his arms. He placed a hand on the back of her head and kissed her deeply, his tongue darting inside her mouth. He used his lips to suck gently on her bottom lip and then to massage her top lip. He skimmed one hand from her breast, where he squeezed her, to her buttocks, where he grabbed her and pulled her into his erection.

"Looks like someone has a little problem of his own," she said, smiling.

"Yes, I do," he said. "Any chance you could help me with it?"

She smiled. He took that as a yes and led her into the bedroom not far from the study. He closed and locked the door and stripped off his clothes then helped her remove hers. He pulled the covers back on the bed and lifted her onto it.

"Now, you shall be treated to another grand experience, my love," he said, as he leaned on one elbow and massaged her buttocks. He found her clitoris with one finger and began to circle it, teasing and plucking at it. Soon, she was spiraling toward a powerful orgasm, her vaginal muscles clenching and unclenching like the fists of a hand. She realized that she had not had a chance to return the favor and reached for his cock.

Her soft hands rubbed up and down the length of him. "Beth! Sweetheart!" he lay back on the bed and blinked his eyes at her, panting as she bent her head to take him in her mouth. She swirled her tongue around the tip of his penis and then took him into her mouth, opening wide so that she didn't scrape him with her teeth. She began to pump him with her hands as she suckled and licked his cock. She felt a surge of power knowing that she could affect him in this way. She cupped his balls and felt him tense with excitement.

She could feel his jism moving up through his cock. "Beth, stop! Stop. I want to come in you." But she did not stop. Before he could get control of his orgasm, he came, spurting into her mouth. She was unprepared for it, but swallowed most of it. He looked at her, panting and dazed at what she'd done.

"Beth," he said, softly, he fell back on the bed and rested, breathing deeply. "That's not the way I wanted things to go," he said, smoothing her hair out of her face. He was still semi-erect; it did not take him long to regain interest. He rose and kneeled between her legs, got a pillow and put it under her buttocks. That opened up her beautiful pussy to his view. She was all soft and pink, light brown and dusty rose colors swirling. Her clitoris sat at attention, its pearly head begging for his attention.

Her pussy was wet; the tissue soft swirls of her labia swollen and waiting for him. He bent down and licked her clitoris and then sucked it between his lips. He kneaded it between his lips, like a small piece of dough. He could feel her legs twitching with each grasp and then flick of his tongue. She was more than ready, but he wanted her to have another strong orgasm before he plunged into her sweet depths.

She wiggled her sweet buttocks as he swirled his tongue around the lips of her sex, sucking and pulling on her. It didn't take long for her to orgasm. He felt her stiffen and then, placing one finger into her pussy, he felt her unravel, her contractions deep and long. "Ramon! Yes. Oh. Yesss." She relaxed and fell back on the bed as he pulled the pillow from under her buttocks. Sweat dotted her brow and she panted, trying to regain her equilibrium.

They held one another, legs wrapped around each other and her head on his chest for a while until he was ready to make love to her again. He kissed her. "Would you like to?" He grabbed his cock and rubbed it suggestively. She licked her lips and nodded to him. He rose again and pulled her up, setting her on her knees so that her buttocks faced him sideways on the bed.

He stepped behind her, standing on the floor. He slapped her buttocks lightly and reached between her legs to finger her clitoris. He kissed her on the buttocks where he'd delivered a slight sting and then kissed up her spine. When he reached her shoulders, he grabbed one of her breasts and flicked the nipple, rolling it between his thumb and forefinger. She began to move in rhythm with his finger.

He positioned his cock at the entrance of her pussy and pushed in; she was tight and wet. Ready for him. He began a slow pistoning motion, rotating his hips as he moved deeper into her warm channel. He reached around her and fingered her clitoris while he moved in and out, in and out, his balls slapping her buttocks as he picked up the pace. They both began to approach orgasm as he made short movements and then long plunges into her. She came first, surprised at the intensity of the orgasm as he pumped his seed into her.

Later, they woke to the soft afternoon sun, shining into the front windows. Ramon stretched and pulled Beth into him. He wondered whether it was too soon to say what was in his heart. Surely she could tell how he felt. Something told him that it was important to let her know what he wanted and how he felt. He reached for her and was surprised to see her eyes open and looking at him.

He kissed her lightly on the lips and went to the restroom to get a warm wet washcloth to clean them both.

"We need to talk, Ramon," Beth said.

"I could not agree more," he said.

"I love what you do to me," she said. "But, surely you must know that this can't. . . This can't." She paused. It felt wrong.

"I don't want to make you feel that we are going to have anything long term," she said. Ramon sat up beside her and pulled her up by lifting her under her arms. She weighed so little that he easily pulled her to him.

"No," he said. She looked at him with a puzzled expression.

"What?" she asked.

"No, you're not going to kill what we obviously have because of your doubts, Beth."

"I'm only saying that there is such a gap in our ages that you should not."

"Just wait one moment," he said. "First of all, I don't want to hear another word about our age difference. It is just an excuse on your part, and you know it, Beth." He allowed the words to sink in for her a while before he spoke again.

"You know how I feel for you," he said, placing a hand over her heart. "I want to marry you. I want us to make a home together. I've loved you since the day I first laid eyes on you." She gasped.

"Nah, ah, No," she said.

"Yes, and you feel something too, Beth. I know you do. You just won't admit it to yourself because you are so worried about what other people will say instead of about your own happiness." She looked at him, her mouth agape, stunned speechless. Beth looked out the window, tears forming at the corners of her eyes. She wiped them, trying not to let him see her face. After a few minutes of consideration, she took a deep breath.

"Ramon, I told you I needed some time," she said. He turned her head to him and kissed her again.

"I know, sweetheart, but I've given you years," he said gently. He smiled. "Life will pass us both by if we don't grab it. Don't let the stupid prejudices of other people ruin what we have. Because," he paused and took a deep breath, "I know that what we have is special." He thought about the unpleasant marriages of some of his friends and their parents. His friends had teased him for the private way that he handled his affairs. His brothers, however, understood him. He had always been the youngest surrounded by those much older than him. He had listened. He had soaked up their love, and he had given it.

10 WATER PLAY

They slept then. Not waking until much later when they smelled the aroma of spicy food wafting up from downstairs. They showered, dressed and went downstairs to be greeted by two other of Ramon's siblings, Isabella and Rosa, who said they were just passing by and wanted to stop in to meet Beth. Ramon and Alejandro gave each other that look. It was highly doubtful that the two women were anything but nosy. But, it had to happen sooner or later. Ramon would rather it be sooner.

Rosa held out a hand to Beth as she rounded the corner into the kitchen.

"Hello, Beth," she said. "Ramon tells me that you two have known each other for quite some time. How is it that we haven't met you before?" She grinned as her older sister came forward too.

"Hi, Beth, Rosa has a tendency to overstate things," said Isabella. "We knew about you but didn't realize we'd actually get to meet you. Ramon is a bit on the quiet side when it comes to his personal life."

"As well he should be, sister," Alejandro said. "A man can't let his sisters know his most heartfelt secrets."

Alejandro winked at Beth and led the group back to the kitchen. Rosa and Isabella had brought large amounts of food from the restaurant. They'd laid it all out on the kitchen island and in the small dining area. They ate with jovial conversation, teasing and recalling childhood incidents. When they finished, they loaded the dishes in the dishwasher and went outside to the deck with wine.

"I think we should get in the pool," Rosa said. "I doubt that you've used it, little brother." Ramon looked at Beth. The others continued talking and teasing.

"Would this bother you, Beth?" Ramon asked. "I know that you. . ."

"No, Ramon, go ahead. I might even join you." His eyebrows rose. "Are you sure? I mean you don't have to do this." She left the group and went upstairs to change into a black bikini. She put a gauzy purple beach wrap on over it. When she arrived, they were investigating the pool area and opening a few windows.

"I'm not going to get in," Beth said. "It's been a while since I've been in a pool. Is it heated?" Ramon nodded.

"You go ahead. I'll watch," Beth said. Ramon and his sisters went upstairs to change. When they came down, Beth was seated a few yards from the pool in a white wicker chair. She leafed through a book. The day was a balmy 69 degrees. Not exactly cold, but not overly warm. The clouds in the sky made it feel a little cooler, so Ramon turned the thermometer up so the water would not be too cold. Isabella and Rosa played water volleyball for a while; Ramon joined them later. Rosa made a few laps across the pool and got out to sit beside Beth. Beth saw a vision of herself surrounded by water and shivered, thinking it was just her old fear nagging at her.

"Aren't you going to get in?" she asked Beth.

"Not today. I, um, I have a little problem with water, large amounts of it, that is."

"I'm sorry to hear that," Rosa said. "Is it serious? I

mean, can you ever get in? Is it an allergic reaction?"

Beth laughed. "No, not quite. My parents died in a boating accident." Beth paused to let that sink in. She felt a little embarrassed that she had blurted out something so personal, but Rosa didn't seem to mind.

"I'm sorry, Beth," she said softly. "How long ago was it?"

"Oh, it was years ago. But I never got over it really. I was very close to my mother. My twin sister and I were teenagers."

"You know, I thought you looked familiar," Rosa said. "Is your sister related to that rich guy, what's his name, Jim Wang or Chen something?" Beth blushed and nodded.

"Um, I don't think she thinks of him that way, though," she said.

"Of course not," Rosa said. "Excuse me for being so forward. I don't often meet people like your sister, so I was surprised to hear that she, uh. ... Well. No matter. Have you and Ramon known each other for a long time?"

Beth explained that they had met on the job and had indeed known each other for a while. She felt that Rosa was fishing for information for a reason. Maybe she was trying to determine whether Ramon was with a woman that was too old for him.

"In case you're wondering, I have told Ramon that he should be with someone his age, but he won't listen," Beth said. Rosa laughed.

"Good luck on getting Ramon to do anything you want him to do," Rosa said. "In fact, if you said black, he would say white. That's just the way he is. He is stubborn." The two women allowed a few minutes of silence to pass. Alejandro walked over to the stereo and turned on Brazilian jazz. He walked to Beth and held out a hand to her. She shook her head, refusing to dance with him.

"Now see, big brother," Ramon said, grinning. "The reason she won't dance with you is that she needs to dance with me first." Without allowing her to refuse him, Ramon rose from the pool and wrapped a towel around himself. He grabbed her hand and pulled her to her feet. "Ramon! You're wet."

"Yes, mamacita, and so are you," he said, laughing and pulling her into him. His sisters and brother prepared to leave as they noted that Beth and Ramon saw nothing but each other. Rosa and Isabella laughed and nudged each other, giving one another that speaking look that said, "Those two are in love." Rosa gestured for the door and pointed at Alejandro. He mouthed, "What?" She frowned and motioned toward the back door of the house.

Ramon realized they were alone as the music became more sultry and dim lights came on to light the pool area. He pulled her toward him so she could feel his erection. "So, Beth," he said. "Are you going to get in the pool with me?"

"I, ah, I, don't like water, Ramon," she said.

"I know, sweetheart," he said. "But sooner or later, you're going to have to get over it. You're surrounded by water."

"Yes, but I don't have to get in it," she said.

He cupped her breast and placed a hand on her buttocks, pulling her into him tighter. "You realize that interesting things can be done in water," he said, whispering into her ear and swaying with her in his arms to the music. The music continued a loop of Brazilian tunes, "The Girl from Ipanema," "No More Blues," "Mas Que Nada" and "Quiet Nights of Quiet Stars." Beth felt herself relaxing, her breasts tingling and that place between her thighs growing warmer and wetter. Before she knew it, Ramon had maneuvered toward the pool and was sitting her down on the edge. He stood between her legs and pulled her to the edge of the pool with her legs dangling in the water. Her heart pounded as he stood there between her legs, holding her close and kissing her. He ran a finger down her neck and across her shoulder, down her arm and then into the band of the top of her swimsuit. She pulled back from him and looked into his eyes. "Relax," he said, and kissed her again. His kisses became deeper as his tongue thrust into her mouth and twined with hers. He wrapped her legs around his waist and pulled her into the water with him. She gasped and tightened her arms around his neck.

"It's OK, sweetheart; nothing is going to happen to you," he said. "See, it's only water. You can stand up in it, but you don't have to, because I have you." He turned around slowly in the water and then put her back on the edge of the pool. He pulled her bathing suit off her and pushed her gently back on the pool floor. He kissed her on each side of her hips, first the right, then the left and then placed a finger in her while he kissed her stomach, then pulled away from her and kissed a trail of hot kisses from her belly button to her clitoris, where he began to suckle her.

Her legs began to flinch as he pulled on her clitoris, sucking it with his lips, pressing it with his tongue and then pinching it with this lips again and again. When he focused devoted attention to that knot of nerves at the tip of her clitoris, Beth began to fall apart. A million stars seemed to shoot through the sky and through her being as the contractions of orgasm surged through her body. She shook with joy and enjoyment. He pulled her to the edge and pressed his engorged cock into her. Already close to coming himself, he withdrew and slammed into her again and again. When his own orgasm hit him with such force that he could not contain his shouts of pleasure, he knew he would never let her go. "Beth, I love you," he said. "I love you." She looked up at him dazed by the confession. She wanted to return the words, but held back. She didn't know whether to say the words to him or not.

Ramon knew not to push her for more. He knew that within Beth a great struggle still existed. That she would need to learn that she could trust him and that he would not take no for an answer. That he would not go away simply because she seemed to think that their ages were an issue. For him, there was no issue. But, he knew, it was time to let her come to see that herself. In time. He could be patient. They panted with the force of their lovemaking. He had pulled himself up on the surface of the pool-room floor beside her, placing a towel over them. After a while, he looked at her and smiled.

"Let's try getting in the water again, chica," he said. She trembled as he pulled her to him again and wrapped her legs around him. Eventually, he let her go. "See," he said, softly. "You can do it. You can get in the water and you can swim." They swam across the short width of the pool together. He dove under her and cupped her mons as she stroked in the water. She came up for air. "Ramon!" She said sputtering. He grinned.

"Try to have fun, Beth," he said, cupping her breasts and pulling her to him again. They played like that for more than an hour. Before long, Ramon had her racing him the length of the pool. When they reached the deep end, he helped her up onto the edge.

"You didn't tell me you were on Olympic swimmer, Beth," he said, smiling at her. "If I'd known how well you can swim, I'd have challenged you way before now."

"You knew from my records that I could swim," she said. "I just haven't enjoyed it for years."

"Is that because of your parents?" he asked, looking down at her.

"Yes," she whispered, the images of her parents drowning flashing in her mind. "They were avid sailors, but a squall arrived quite unexpectedly and they were caught unaware."

Then she whispered: "They were both good swimmers, but they just didn't make it."

"Is that why you don't want to get in the water?" he

asked. She said nothing. He put a finger under her chin and looked in her eyes. "Beth, you realize that it was an accident. Most people go out and come home just fine. Some people die in car accidents just as well as on the water. It happens. I'm sorry it happened to your parents, but they would not want you to be afraid of something they loved so much."

Beth sat there as though she were looking into the distance. A dog barked in the neighborhood. There was the creaking of a screen backdoor and then a slam. A car door slammed. Birds whistled and tweeted. Cars rolled by quietly in the distance. The horn of a ship crooned off the bay side of the island. The water in the pool lapped against the sides. The dim lights gave everything a shadowy look. He pulled her into his arms and hugged her tight.

11 KIDNAPPED

Arnold Dickens prided himself on having the right equipment. With the right equipment, any job could be done. He had had a man follow the bitch to her lover's house. He could tell by looking at her that she was afraid of water, afraid to dive into that pool the others were so happily using. They really were so stupid, allowing anyone to see into their lives with that clear paned glass around the swimming pool area. The trees blocked some of the view, but not all of it. She had a habit of wearing purple whenever she went out. That seemed to be her favorite color.

He knew he'd be able to tell her from the sister who looked so much like her. His men had made a mistake the other night thinking she was nearby but out of the house. It was her sister who was next door visiting a friend, not Beth. But the little idiots didn't look closely. Now, they knew better. He told them to always watch for something purple on the twin they wanted. She was well guarded; he saw the extra security guards the boyfriend had placed in the neighborhood, but soon, they would relax, grow careless. Then, he would have his chance. He had rented a house for sale nearby. Anything could be had for the right price. No one would suspect that he didn't belong in the neighborhood.

All it took was a little patience. She was dressed in a black swimming suit with a purple beach skirt around her waist. Her plump little breasts pebbled through her top. Arnold was growing hard watching her through his scope. No need to kill the hot little piece. That fool from back east he had assigned only needed to get the computer equipment, but he couldn't even do that. Arnold sighed. You know the old saying, he thought: If you want something done, do it yourself. That's what he was going to have to do, with a little help, of course. He licked his lips.

His tight jeans made it impossible for him to get comfortable. He unzipped his fly and let his cock hang out; it was painfully hard. He was going to take her right from under their noses. It wouldn't be difficult. If he could get her and her computer, he could make certain he got to whatever it was that agent wanted on her computer. Then, he would stuff his cock into her. He couldn't wait. He took himself in hand.

Zah soon found the culprit in the mystery about codes and missing agents. Her mathematical abilities far exceeded the average techie's. While Beth was good, she wasn't as good as Zah. Zah smiled as she finished her analysis.

"Son of a ... ," she said under her breath. "This could solve many problems." She contacted the contractor high in the food chain and let him know that she'd found something interesting, not only interesting but quite valuable, in the McKean records. It didn't take him long to arrive at her place, where there were adequate security measures in place to protect the data. She copied the data to a travel drive, and then she'd cleaned Beth's computer of the incriminating data. There would be nothing there for anyone to discover.

Then she rethought things. No, there should be something there. She put a bogus file with a code that looked similar to what she'd removed and copied it to all existing drives on Beth's computer. When Daxton walked in to her condo, she was sitting with her back to him. She'd watched, on her camera, as he walked up the steps and into her apartment. She only needed to press an icon on her phone to let him in.

"Hey, sweet cakes," he said, walking up behind her. She was dressed in black leather pants and had tattoos in interesting places. They had had a fuck buddy relationship going for some time. She was short but a bit too skinny for his tastes. But he loved the way she felt when he pinned her down for a good fuck. She knew what he wanted and wanted it too. A woman who spent most of her time with her head buried in a computer screen got needy occasionally. She lacked for human interaction and welcomed the hard, pounding sex.

He was all muscle, a dedicated weight lifter and athlete. He stood nearly two feet taller. He placed his gun on the table beside her bed and stripped out of his jeans and his collared shirt. He never bothered with underclothes. She wore a black lace top that barely covered her sweet tits. He helped her get her leather pants off and then ripped her lacy top off. He lifted her in his arms and helped her wrap her legs around his waist.

"Miss me?" he asked. She nipped at his lips with her sharp white teeth.

"What do you think, you goofball?" she said, rubbing her sex against him.

He could feel her wetness. "Hmm, already, princess? You get in the mood fast."

"I've been waiting for you for too long. Let's get with it." He pressed her to the wall and placed his large cock at her entrance and surged into her. She was tight and wet. Fuck, she was good. He stayed still inside her to give her a chance to grow accustomed to his girth, meanwhile he kissed her on her forehead, lips, cheeks and neck. "Dax, please!" That was all it took. He pulled out of her and slammed back in, beginning a relentless pounding that drove them both to the height of orgasm. When he came inside her, he could feel her pussy clinching like a tight fist around him. They both fell to the bed, panting and laughing.

"Your cunt is going to kill me someday," he said.

"Oh yeah. Well, if that's the way it's going to be, I'd better get my use out of you before you keel over from excess pussy enjoyment," she laughed.

"Mmm. Let's have a little more of that excess," he said, pulling her to him again. They made love like that into the night and part of the morning. Between fucking, Zah told Dax what she'd discovered about the coding in Beth's computer. He looked it over and whistled through his teeth.

"This is too hot for either of you, sweetheart," he said. "I'll take it off your hands."

"Oops," she said, holding the travel drive away from him. "One more time." She grinned; he grabbed her by her buttocks and they were at it again. When Dax left her condo later that day, he'd assured her that Beth would get some protection, but it would not be of the physical variety as no one could be spared at the time. However, he was certain she was safe enough for the time being. He assured Zah that any fallout would probably not come down on Beth or Zah for discovering the sensitive information. Before he left, he checked Zah's equipment to be sure it was clean. "Until next time, sweet cakes," he said, bending down to give her a kiss. "Hey, why don't we make this a regular thing?" Was he hinting at marriage?

"You wish," she said, and pushed him toward the door.

"Hey, Gina," Beth said, after pushing the speaker button on her cell phone. She had gone up to the bedroom she had been given at Ramon's house and had just finished taking a shower when Gina called.

"How are things going for you, Beth?" Gina asked. She waited a moment for Beth to respond.

"I met Ramon's sisters and another brother," Beth said.

"Wow, looks like you'll have met the entire family soon," Gina said. "This sounds serious." Beth didn't comment further. Gina and Mateo had talked about his large family and had shared some of the challenges he thought Ramon faced with his mother. But Gina didn't want to talk about that.

"I had a dream last night," Gina said. "I want to talk to you about it but not over the phone. I thought I'd bring you your car, and we could go out for a bite to eat or something."

"Sounds like a plan," Beth said. They agreed to meet in front of Ramon's house. Beth dressed in a thin sweater, pair of jeans and boots. She wrapped a violet scarf around her neck and put on silver earrings. She looked at some of the tools of her profession when she put together her things. Her boots had a hidden blade in them; a small gun was hidden in her purse. She decided to leave her larger weapon at Ramon's and carried a smaller gun hidden on her hip.

She considered whether she should take the computer with her, but instead, fingered the travel drive poking from its port; it had all she needed on it. She knew Zah would have protected everything on the computer by now. She ejected the travel drive from the computer and stuffed it in a jean pocket. The dream that Gina had had was probably a premonition of some sort. She had been feeling weird lately herself, as though someone was watching her. She pulled out her lip-gloss and smoothed it on, bending down in the mirror to get a look. The doorbell rang downstairs as she reached in the closet for a coat. Could that be Gina already?

Just as she was about to head out of the bedroom door, her computer dinged. It was Zah. She got online to see what Zah had to say about her findings.

Ramon was checking the pH level on the pool water when Alejandro came to say there was someone at the door waiting to speak to him. "Who is it?" Ramon asked, pulling a T-shirt over his head and past his rippling abs. Alejandro shrugged and ducked into the kitchen as though he had something important to do. When Ramon arrived at the door, he couldn't believe what he was seeing. Barbara stood there, a little older than when they'd been together, but just as curvy as she'd been when he was a teen. He swallowed hard and looked upstairs to where Beth was.

"Uh, Barbara," he smiled. "What brings you here? How did you find where I live?"

"No, 'I'm thrilled to see you, Barbara.' 'I was just coming to see you, Barbara,'" she said, smirking. Ramon heard Beth moving about upstairs and stepped out onto the front porch.

"Ah, yes," he said, looking down. This could get awkward. He didn't want Beth to think that he was seeing someone else. At the same time, he didn't want Barbara to think he had no consideration or appreciation for what she'd done for him in the past. Still, it could get awkward if he had to make introductions between the two as he had no intention whatsoever of starting up something with Barbara again. She had golden skin and curly dark brown hair. Her large breasts poked out at him as though inviting him to wrap his hands around them. She wore a tight black dress that hugged her curves and made her buttocks seem much larger than they were. He realized as he took another look at her that the feelings he had for her years ago were gone. There was not the slightest stir in him. He had to make her understand.

"Barbara," he said, looking both ways up and down

the street. "Let's go to your car. I need to talk to you."

Beth arrived at the front door and paused. Should she tell someone where she was going? She looked in the kitchen and found no one there. She shrugged and wrote a note using a piece of paper and a pen she found on a hallway table. She set it on the table in a tent form with Ramon's name on it. She heard some scraping in the back but dismissed it as Alejandro. When she arrived on the small porch at the front of the house, she could see her sister had parked her car further to the west of the house. She saw two people sitting in a car further up the street but couldn't make out who they were, so she slipped off the porch and walked swiftly to her sister.

"Took you long enough," Gina said smiling at her and giving her a quick hug. "What were you doing?"

"I was already to go when Zah pinged me, saying that they had found the codes and had done some work to fix things," Beth said.

"Yeah, so, does this mean you're off the hook for this mess?" Gina asked.

"No, I don't think so, not entirely," Beth said. "I think I'll have some explaining to do, but it goes a long way toward giving me some protection that I have someone helping to sort out things. Where are we going for a snack?"

"The Mod."

They drove there in a tense silence, listening to the satellite radio on the way. Gina broke the tension. "So are you going to meet the mother, you think?"

Beth sighed. "I don't think I should, Gina. I've told Ramon that it's no good. I'm too old for him. But he insists that things will be all right. I think he wants me to meet everyone in his family. I just can't see that it can work."

"Aren't you being a little pessimistic, Beth? I mean, if Ramon seems to know what he wants and you seem to want to be with him, isn't that all that matters?"

"You would think so, but he comes from a big family of husbands and wives with children. It just doesn't seem to be something that we can do. I mean. I can't have children at this age, I don't think."

"Why not?" Beth looked at Gina. She was turning left on to 25th Street toward The Strand. Beth held her breath and looked at Gina as though she were a two-headed alien.

"Gina, that's just foolish talk, and you know it."

"Why is it? There have been reports of women in their 50s having children. Some of them borrow an egg from a younger woman to do it, but it's doable."

"I'm not having this conversation with you, Gina." Beth looked off to the side.

"Why not? You think it's ridiculous? That's it? Oh, maybe you're just chicken." Beth placed a hand on her forehead and rubbed it and then rubbed her eyes.

"Right, and by the time my children are 20 I'd be maybe in my 70s — if I live that long."

"So, you're afraid to try so that you never give it a chance. I didn't take you for that much of a coward, Beth," Gina said. "But you're right. There's no point in discussing it if you're going to be so pessimistic that you don't even give the two of you a chance. If the man loves you and you love him. . ." Gina looked at her again. She was stopped at a light on Broadway and 25th Street.

"OK, I think we've jumped over a big question here," said Gina. "Do you love him?"

"Yes," Beth said in a whisper.

"What?" Gina cupped a hand to her ear. "I didn't hear you."

"Yes!" Beth shouted. "I do. I just. I'm not ready to commit. I'm just not ready yet."

"Well, that settles everything then," her sister said, smiling. "Everything will work out. You'll see. I guess you haven't told him." Beth glared at her.

"I'm not talking about this with you, Gina. Let's move

on." The two women talked of Gina's son and his budding romance overseas. But they did not return to Ramon and Beth. When they were parked and settled at the back room of the Mod with coffee, the two women resumed talking in more polite tones.

"So what was it you wanted to tell me really, Gina?" Beth asked. "You said you had a disturbing dream."

"Yes," Gina said, taking a sip of her coffee. "I dreamed that you were on a boat, the same one that Mom and Dad had." Gina stopped and took another gulp of her coffee. Beth closed her eyes and drank several swallows of her own coffee.

"It's time we get it out there in the open," Beth said. "I think I know what you dreamed. I've been sensing some disturbing visions myself."

"What do you think it means?" Gina asked.

"I hope it doesn't mean that I'm going to have to deal with some large body of water." She paused and looked out at the street. They were sitting in the large room to the east of the baristas where customers sat in overstuffed chairs with their computers or notebooks before them. They rarely looked up. Beth and Gina sat at a table toward the back. Business was not brisk at this hour, so they had plenty of space between them and other customers. Colorful paintings decorated the walls, tagged with prices for the artist's work. Every now and then, a customer got up to use the bathroom behind their table.

"I think it means that something is about to happen and that you need to be ready, Beth," Gina said. "What exactly is going on? You never gave me much of an explanation after that incident at my house."

"Sorry," Beth winced. "I've been rather preoccupied. But I suppose Mateo filled you in on some of it?"

"He told me only what Ramon told him, and that wasn't much," Gina said, sipping at her coffee. A woman walked in who knew Gina and waved at her. The woman sat in one of the large chairs across the room.

"That's Wendy from school," Gina said. "You remember her?" Beth looked over and smiled at the woman.

"No, not really; I don't have a social media account, so I don't keep in touch with our class," Beth said. Wendy sat her things down and came over to visit the two women. They exchanged small talk, and Beth took Wendy's number, promising to give her a call later.

"She's really a nice woman," Gina said. "I think she had been a bit of a gossip in high school, but she's pretty much a loner now."

Then, after a pause, Gina asked: "So are you going to tell me what really has been happening or what?"

"Let's walk," Beth said.

"I like your scarf," Gina said, fingering the lavender material. Beth took it from around her neck and put it on her sister. "Here," Beth said, smiling. The two sisters long had a habit of trading clothes. "You take it." Gina fingered the brooch that was attached to the scarf. It was blue and purple, with sparkling chips of glass and crystal and spiked spindles in the shape of a flower. "Are you sure? The scarf and the broach? They're so pretty," Gina said. Beth smiled and nodded. There was no need for further conversation on the matter. Their habits of gift giving to one another were nothing unusual. They took their cups to the cupboard in the main room and left the café. They headed toward The Strand.

"So, you know about the attack on Aunt Maddy and Uncle Gerald," Beth said, pausing as a passerby swerved to avoid them.

"Recall that I explained to you the reason for my investigation of the McKeans' disappearance." Gina nodded, her forehead furrowing with concern as she listened. "It appears that they had some special codes on their devices that I was unaware of when I copied some of their files. I decided that there might be some hint about where they'd gone or what happened to them, so my plan was to go through everything carefully and to get one of my cyber friends to help me with the review. But before I could get very far with it, of course, Ramon showed up and we went for a date."

"You don't think Ramon had anything to do with this do you?" Gina asked.

"No," Beth said emphatically. "He's been working with me to see whether we can find out who's behind these attempts on my life." Gina shuddered, a chill going through her.

"Now that you put it that way," Gina said. "It seems like this is a matter for the police. Why don't the two of you have them involved? Perhaps a detective or someone at the agency could help you."

"If my guess is right, my friend might have those bases covered already. Besides which, Ramon has a family full of astute brothers who are helping, as you know." They stopped at the corner where a bank building sat and waited for traffic to go by. "Let's cut through the bank building parking lot." Gina looked at her askew and then nodded, realizing that it was another way of protecting their conversation.

"So, there was an attempt on my life that night, at about the same time someone was trying to steal some of the travel drives from your house," Beth said.

"Why don't you just give them what they want?" Gina asked.

"Good question, but until I know who they are, what the codes do and why they want the codes, I can't just hand them over. The codes could do something that we don't want done. So, I've arranged for someone higher up on the food chain to take over."

Just then a van came speeding into the garage and screeched to a halt beside the two women. Gina was frozen in place, but Beth realized at once that this was an abduction attempt. She grabbed her sister's hand and tugged her back, away from the van. But she wasn't fast enough; two men dressed in coveralls and ski masks grabbed both sisters and tossed them into the van. They subdued both women with a punch to the face; then one of the men placed duct tape over their mouths. They both were covered with a burlap sack and had their hands and feet tied. Their cell phones were taken. Beth felt herself sinking into darkness as the van sped off and out of the driveway of the garage. Her last thought was of her sister and then of Ramon. Would he find them in time?

12 THE TROUBLE WITH TWINS

Arnold told the two he had working for him, Cullen and Logan, that they had better not mess this up. So, Cullen had the presence of mind to grab both women. "Hey, boss," he said. "We got both of 'em. What do you want us to do with 'em? We didn't expect both." Arnold told him to keep both women and proceed with their original plan. Arnold had explained again and again that the two women were twins and that Cullen and Logan needed to watch for something special, like the color purple, but both women were wearing something in that color. Cullen looked down at one of them.

One was wearing a purple scarf; the other was wearing a shirt that looked like the color purple to him. What Arnold didn't realize was that Cullen was color-blind. What looked like red to other people was actually purple for Cullen. One sister was wearing a deep dark burgundy. It was close enough. But, he wasn't going to take any chances; he had screwed this up before. He had tried to hurt the bitch that Arnold sent him after on The Strand, but that man with her had saved her.

The idea was to make her sloppy and make her tip off where she put her stuff — to distract her. But it hadn't worked. They didn't figure on the fuckin' hero with her. Eventually, they'd probably have to take care of him too. Cullen pulled the burlap bag off Beth and Gina. He checked their pockets and was surprised to find that one of them had a knife in her boot and a gun on her hip. This must be the one, he thought, the one with the knife and gun on her. He disarmed Beth and finished patting both women down and took the opportunity to fondle them. His hard on was uncomfortable, but he couldn't quite get fully excited at a woman who was incapacitated. He liked a woman who was awake. It was more fun that way. He wanted them to struggle. Logan looked back at Cullen from the driver's seat. "Hey, leave some for me," he said.

"There's not going to be any leavings," Cullen said. "We're taking them exactly where the boss wants them." He moved to the front seat to give Logan directions.

"Why do we need both of them?"

"Look, don't ask questions. I have no idea what he wants with this one," he said, pointing at Beth. "She looks pretty sweet to me." Cullen rubbed at his crotch. "They both do. Hurry up and get us there. We don't want no fuckups."

Beth was conscious long before this fool had begun fondling her and her sister. She tried a trick she and Gina played often when they were children. They played at thinking thoughts that they wanted the other to know without saying the words. So she concentrated and thought: "Don't open your eyes, Gina. When the van stops, make a run for it. Get help." She figured she could fight off one or both, but Gina was not trained for any of this. While her wrists were bound, her fingers were free. She used them to loosen Gina's bonds. After a twenty-minute drive, the dark gray van bounced over rutted holes and pulled up to a small pier for boats. They pulled the van around and backed it up to the pier. It was dark by the time they reached the pier.

Confident that both women were out cold, Cullen left the van's back door open while he went to the boat to get the length of black canvas he planned to wrap one of the women in. He would have to secure her and come back to get the other woman. He looked over at the small bait shop and beer stand to see whether there was anyone coming their way. All was quiet. No one was in the parking area. If there were people around, they were all in the bait shop. Logan walked the short distance to the bait shop to get some beer. When Cullen came back, one of the bodies was gone. Cullen assumed that Logan had moved the other woman and shrugged. Seeing a lump of something black on the boat, he felt sure that this was the other woman.

Logan loaded the beer and snacks on the boat. They had placed a one-person kayak in the Cuddy boat so that one of them could row back if necessary. Cullen checked the woman left in the van again. She seemed to be coming to; he felt her buttocks and around her hips and noticed a slight bulge. There was a travel drive in her pocket. He dug it out of her pocket and whistled. Logan came around to the back of the van. "What did you find?" he asked. Cullen held out the travel drive.

"Get this back to Arnold as fast as you can. We might not have to ransom the bitches for what he wants from them. This might be what he's looking for," he said.

"Are you going to take them out on the bay?" Logan asked.

"Yeah, that's what the man said he wanted us to do, but take him that drive and hide the van so that no one can find it. Then, find a way to meet me out there."

"I'm not going to find a skiff and come looking for you, man," Logan said. "I'm finished with this shit." Cullen grabbed his T-shirt.

"Look, dirt bag," he paused, looking down at the woman who was squirming on the floor of the van. It looked like she'd been working on the rope around her hands. He cuffed her on the head again and flipped her over, placing a knee in the small of her back to keep her still. "We don't get paid until we deliver what he wants, and personally, I'm not going to fuck it up because I need the money. You get it?" Cullen glared at Logan, his hands fisting at his sides.

"I didn't get into this to do nothing to women," Logan said. "He didn't say kill them, did he?" Cullen slapped Logan in the head. The force of the hit was enough to make Logan lose his balance and land partly in the water behind the van and partly on the rough rocks of the ramp. Logan regained his feet and stood up quickly; he wanted to punch Cullen but he knew what Cullen was capable of doing. Cullen had a Ruger strapped to his hip; that was enough to make Logan rethink what he wanted to do. He wiped blood from his lip and held out his hand for the travel drive, a small black rectangle about two inches long. He tucked it in his pants.

"Fine, Cullen," he said, his chest heaving from his anger and frustration. "Just remember that if you need someone to watch your back, it's no longer going to be me."

"I'll remember to look for someone with a little more backbone than you," Cullen said. "While you're taking care of the van, I'm going to have some fun with these two bitches. Now, get out of here and take that thing to Arnold."

Logan stalked off to the front of the van and waited for Cullen to finish loading the last woman into the small cabin of the boat. When Cullen slammed the van door, Logan pressed hard on the gas and skidded in the gravel and rocks, taking off out of the parking lot.

13 LOVE AND MARRIAGE

Ramon sat in the car with Barbara hoping that she would understand what he was trying to explain. He'd said it twice already, but she didn't seem to want to accept it. They hadn't been together in years. Before he'd met Beth, it wasn't unusual for him to look her up when he came to town. But that was nearly eight years ago. How could she think that he would want to pick up where they left off — that there would be no changes in his life?

He decided to change tactics. Maybe if he showed some interest in what was going on in her life, she would come to understand that too much time had passed for them to have an affair again.

"Barbara, what has been going on in your life since I left?" he asked, turning his head to look at her. It was getting dark outside and he had been looking at the children riding their bikes in the street and playing ball.

"It's not like I haven't had anyone to be with," she said

defensively, holding her chin up. "I had a boyfriend for a while." She paused, taking a breath. "Someone my age." She was nearly 60 by now, he thought.

His voice softened. "Was he good to you?" She gasped.

"He died."

"Oh, Barbara," he said, taking her in his arms. "I'm so sorry." She sobbed.

"Was it recent?" he asked.

"About four years ago," she said. Suddenly, he wondered whether Barbara was playing him, like a cat with a mouse. He backed away from her as though he was scalded and looked into her face. She seemed to be composing her expressions and no real tears were falling from her eyes. He breathed deeply.

"Barbara, what of your family? You have a daughter and niece, right? Do you visit with them?"

"Oh yeah," she said. "I see them quite a bit. But it's not like being with you, Ramon. Can't you see what I'm trying to say? Can't we just start seeing each other again and see how it goes?" Several moments passed as Ramon looked out in the distance. Something was bothering him but he couldn't quite put his finger on it. He frowned. Something wasn't right with Beth. He turned and looked at the house. There was a lamp on upstairs where they shared a room. He knew he had to end this quickly and cleanly so that he could move on with his life. He turned his head back to face Barbara.

"Barbara, I can't be with you. I . . . uh. There's someone else in my life." Suddenly, Barbara began to scream.

"Noooooo. . . You can't. Noooo." Her body shook with rage. She reached over to him, hit him in the chest and tried to scratch his face. "No, you can't do this, Ramon; I won't let you." This time, real tears were cascading down her face. He grabbed her hands to keep her from hurting him. He waited a moment for her to calm down and said in almost a whisper.

"Barbara, you can't get me back that way. As a matter of fact, there is no way we're going to be a couple again. I love her." She stilled and looked at him with wide eyes.

"You love. You, you. You love her?"

"Yes, I do. I'm going to marry her." Barbara sniffed. He handed her a handkerchief. He was a bit stunned that he'd said the words out loud and a little disappointed in himself for saying them to Barbara.

"She's your age, isn't she?" she prodded, pouting and belligerent. "I knew it. I knew you would find someone your own age after you used me for your own fun."

"Barbara, that's not the way it was for us, and you know it," he said. They had long ago agreed that Ramon had to find his way in the world, to figure out what he wanted to do with his life, to leave his family behind and strike out on his own. He remembered that day when they had said their goodbyes. He thought he'd never see Barbara again. Again, he felt something urgent tugging at his consciousness, as though Beth was trying to say something to him.

Barbara sniffled and hiccoughed as though she could wring more time from the moment with a bid for his sympathy. But the urgency for him to get away was even more pressing.

"Barbara, I'm telling you this once. I'm sorry that I have to be so short but I have something important to do. If you ever loved me, I think you would want me to be happy, and I am. So, this is it. We are not going to be a couple again. It is not going to happen. You were sweet and good to me. I learned a great deal from you, but it's over. My life has moved on, and you were one of the important people in my life when you were in it. But I have found someone who is very dear to me — the me I am now." He stopped talking as he noticed Alejandro walking out of the front door looking harried. He got out of Barbara's car and bent down so he could see her in the driver's seat. He held out his hand to her. "Barbara, don't give up on finding someone to be with, someone who will make you happy," he said. He held out his hand to shake hers, but she turned from him and started her car. He shut the door, and she sped off. He looked at her retreating vehicle and inhaled deeply. He turned and faced Alejandro.

Alejandro placed a hand on his shoulder. "Little brother, you do have a knack for getting into trouble, but I think you have a more pressing problem right now. Beth is gone." Ramon felt a kick in the gut and a chill in his spine.

The two checked the house thoroughly and found the note Beth had left on the hall table. "Damn!" Ramon said, running a hand through his hair. "I should have stayed with her every minute." He took out his cell phone and tried calling her. No answer. He had her number plugged into an app on his cell phone that would tell him where she was. The number indicated that she, or her cell phone at least, was somewhere near the Pelican Island bridge. He doubted that she was there as she would have little reason to go there. He peered at his phone as it hit him. She had been abducted. He raced to her computer and logged on. He tried sending a note to Zah telling her that Beth might have been abducted and that he would need some agency help. He looked around for a remote key fob.

Her note said she had gone to the Mod with her sister, and that her sister was returning her car; he knew she had a second fob for her car somewhere. If he could locate it fast, he could tell whether she had been taken in her car or in some other vehicle. He found the key fob in her luggage. Beth was neat and prepared for emergencies. He pocketed the fob and his iPad and phone and raced downstairs to meet Alejandro in the hall.

He had pictures of Beth on his cell phone. Maybe he could start there. But first, he called Gina. There was no answer on her phone either. He and Alejandro called Mateo, letting him know what happened. Mateo had planned to pick up Gina at Ramon's house after Gina called him, but he had received no call.

"We can't reach either sister," Ramon told Mateo over the phone. "Check Gina's house thoroughly and then the neighbors' houses. Check the area; then text me to let me know what you found. Stay there in case they come to Gina's house."

Alejandro and Ramon walked into the Mod and showed pictures around the café. A woman named Wendy in the east room said she'd spoken to Gina and Beth at about 6 p.m. and that the two women had headed out of the café headed west. Ramon and Alejandro split up. Alejandro checked the blocks along Postoffice Street and saw no evidence that the women had parked there. They checked a bank parking lot at the end of the street and then headed toward the Frost Bank parking lot. There, an attendant said that two women had been seen walking in the lot and that there had been two men with them. She couldn't see what happened next as the booth faced east, and the conflict seemed to be occurring in the back of the lot.

"Did you call the police?" Alejandro asked.

"Yes, but they were long gone by the time the cops got here," she said. "I didn't see any blood or anything. It happened so fast."

"Is there a security camera where we could view what happened?" Ramon asked. He told her that he worked for a law enforcement agency and flashed an old ID.

"Yes, but the manager for that doesn't get back to the building until the morning, after 10," she said. Ramon cursed and looked back toward the parking lot's west end. He thanked the woman and turned his attention to finding Beth's vehicle. They found it not far from the bank building, in the next block. There was no indication that either woman had made it to the car.

"Looks like we're back where we started," Alejandro said. "We need to see whether we can get the local cops involved. Ramon stood on the sidewalk near the car, thinking. He didn't want to complicate matters by getting the local authorities involved. Beth's safety was the issue, so he'd have to find her and get her out of harm's way before the agency or the police found out what was happening.

"Let's go back to the car attendant and ask her some more questions about the type of vehicle that was here," Ramon said. The two asked the woman a few more questions, finding out that the van was dark, maybe black or charcoal gray. The van had headed west on Market Street. That was a start. Ramon tried to think what other tools were at his disposal for tracking the women. They returned to the Mod where an Internet connection made it easier for him to use the app that tracked Beth's cell phone. He retrieved his iPad from his car and tracked her phone again. The history of her phone indicated that they had stopped here at the Mod, then gone to the bank parking lot. The phone's chip signal seemed to pause at some point. Maybe they had tried to destroy the phone. But Beth's phone had a special element that allowed it to be tracked. He picked up the signal again. It was headed toward the West End and ended at . . . He cursed again. He looked at Alejandro.

"I think they might have taken both women out on the bay," he said, a shudder going through him. Beth's fear of water would make it difficult for her to overcome any circumstances involved in her abduction. She had been trained to fight, and to bring psychology to bear in these circumstances. But why had they taken her? What did they hope to accomplish? Did they want to ransom her for the computer codes? That must be it. He shook his head in dismay. This kidnapper, whoever he was, was going to draw the agency to him by doing this. He must be desperate. How would he cope with the loss of Beth? If he lost her, his life would never be the same. No, he simply would not have a life. He wondered whether he could pray. It had been a long time. He hadn't even given it any thought. But now, it was something he wished he'd had a lot more practice doing.

Gina hid behind the cars in the rough parking lot until the van had pulled away from the ramp. Then the boat started and pulled out into the bay. Her heart sank as she realized her twin was on that boat and that Beth was depending on her to find a way to help. There hadn't been enough time for her to free Beth. She looked over at the bait shop; there were mostly drunks in there. Her house was just down the road, and Beth had said she did not want the police involved. There was some issue with Beth's involvement in this mess. She would try first to get help from Ramon.

Her house was not far away. She breathed heavily, her heart thumping against her chest. The large gravel and rocks bit into the soles of her thin shoes. She had not worn her athletic shoes. It was dark out here and only one streetlight shone at the end of the lot. She made her way to the corner and ducked behind a large plant when a car approached. If it was Logan, coming back because he realized she wasn't on the boat, she would need to find a way to get to her house without being seen. As it was, it was one of her neighbors, who stopped her car and offered Gina a ride, taking her right to her front door.

The door was locked, and Gina didn't have her keys, so she went around to the side door. It was easily opened because it had not been repaired from the break-in. She walked in and went to her landline phone. She thought of calling Ramon but realized that if she even had his phone number, it was on her cell phone, which had been taken by the abductors. Mateo was not there. Where was he? She raced upstairs to check; then went next door to her aunt and uncle's house. They were not home either. Where was everybody? Her hands began to shake as she realized that time was important. Her sister was at risk, and she needed help soon, or they might not find Beth. Just then, the sliding glass door opened slowly and Mateo walked in. Gina had been holding her breath and was prepared to grab a knife as the door opened.

"Mateo!" she ran to him and hugged him. She began to tell him what happened.

"Beth and I we were. … Some man. Two men. They took us. Beth is still," she said, stuttering and struggling to get out the words. She breathed heavily and tried to catch her breath, but she was shaking so hard she could hardly compose herself.

"I know," Mateo said.

"You know!" she screamed.

"Yes, calm down. Ramon called me to say he thought the two of you had been taken. Give me a minute to call him, and then we can figure out what's going on." Mateo called Ramon to tell him that Gina was there and that Beth was still with the kidnappers. It seemed only minutes before Ramon and Alejandro walked in the door. By then, Aunt Maddy and Uncle Gerald were there too.

"OK, Gina," Ramon said. "You're very important to finding Beth because we can't let them get too far from shore with her. Can you tell us about the kind of boat they were using?"

"It was white," she said. Ramon rolled his eyes and took a deep breath.

"Most of them are, but can you tell us about what size it was and what shape?"

"I don't know!" Gina shouted. "Find my sister. Just find her!" Tears streamed down her face, and her aunt came and folded her in her arms. Aunt Maddy had a go at it.

"Everything is going to be fine," Aunt Maddy said, looking into Gina's eyes. "We won't let them hurt your sister." Gina shook with her terror. Maddy tried her best to soothe her, rubbing her back and offering her water.

"Gerald, go get that book about boats that you have in your library and bring it back here," Aunt Maddy said in a commanding voice. "You," she said, pointing to Mateo, "Go get flashlights from the garage under Gina's house. You, yes, you, Alejandro, is it?" she asked, though it was more like a statement. "Go to the end of the pier and see whether Gerald's little boat has gas in it. If not, go get some more at that little place down at the end of the street. Mateo, go tell Gerald that we will need his night vision scope," she said. Ramon stood there in awe. Maddy was as cool as they came. If this was the family he would be marrying into, he would never have to worry about safety. This woman was fearless.

Gerald handed the book on boats to Ramon and they sat Gina down on the couch with the book before her. "Gina," he said, after Maddy had helped her concentrate on the book. "Let's narrow down what kind of boat Beth is on."

"Do you think that she is still on the boat? Do you think they might have?" she broke up again, sobbing. Maddy took her by the shoulders and shook her.

"Look, Gina, pull yourself together," Maddy said. "We can't find her if you don't concentrate." Ramon was pulling the book closer. Alejandro turned on another light and they helped her narrow it down to a Cuddy.

"So the boat had a cover of some sort," Ramon said. "A storage area. That gives us some good information." Her eyes and nose were red, and she sniffled, trying again to calm herself.

"I feel her. She's not far," Gina said. Ramon looked at Alejandro and Mateo. They all exchanged glances that seemed to imply that they thought she had gone off the deep end. "I have a viewing area … a cupola where we can see. I use it for birding. We can look, find her," Gina said, her hands shaking as she got up to lead the way to the top of her house. She had not imagined when she had her husband design the cupola as a viewing station for birding that it would be so important.

When Ramon and Alejandro got to the cupola with Gina, they sent her back down with Mateo. She was too upset to help and they needed quiet and concentration. They began to view the horizon. There were few craft out on the water at this time of night, but there were some shadows. The moon was nearly full, so there was some natural light. The night vision scope helped them to make out a small craft that might be a Cuddy boat to the far west of the bay. Alejandro was looking west using the scope.

"Gotcha," he whispered and handed the scope to Ramon, who was using a pair of regular binoculars. "That's got to be it."

"You're right, Alejandro. Whoever is driving it is trying not to be seen. He just turned off the lights and the engine. We've got to get there."

14 FACING FEARS

There were few times when Beth had had to use her training as an agent. She really had not had to use much of it at all. She remained calm and collected as she sensed the environment. The ignition of the boat was near where she'd been unceremoniously stashed out of the way. The abductor, whoever he was, thought she was still unconscious. Soon, though, he slowed the boat to a stop and fished around in a sack for some beer and turned the engine off. He walked to the stern of the boat, obviously intent on waiting for instructions. She heard the sound of a beer can snap and then the gulping sounds of Cullen drinking. His phone rang. He fished it out of his back pocket and spoke to someone on the other end.

"Yeah," he said. "I'll be home as soon as I can. No, don't wait up for me. Put your mother on the phone." Silence while he listened. "No, we're not goin' over old ground. I want you out of the house when I get home, bitch. I told you. No, it's not goin' to happen." More silence. He got up and paced in the small area of the boat. "No, I told you. That woman and me have a thing goin' way back. Yeah. She is. No, I'm not gonna stop seeing her. You ain't gonna stop seeing your girlfriend." Soon, his voice drifted off and he ended the call. Soon after, the phone rang again and he walked away from the prow and toward the stern; he was speaking in a low voice, standing at the back of the boat.

"Yeah," he said. "I've got both of them. I sent him with what you needed," he said. Long moment of silence. "That's not my fault then is it. . . . Yeah. I'll check again. It's dark out here, man. She ain't got anything else on her."

Ah. This conversation was getting interesting. Beth realized that Cullen was distracted and agitated. He hadn't realized that Gina was gone. Good. She wondered who this clutz was working for — a Russian agent? Maybe he was working for some mobster. Her eyes had grown accustomed to the light. She noticed that an electrical line was not far from her head. Perhaps it connected to the ignition switch. She followed the wire with her eyes. If she could cut the wire to the ignition, that would keep him from taking the boat further out into the bay.

Though her hands were tied at the wrists, her fingers were free. She was able to turn over quietly so that she could move her hands to her side, where she had a very thin blade hidden in the seam of her jeans. She was able to shimmy it out and clip the wire, but the blade fell down into the bowels of the boat. As it pinged, she flinched, hoping he had not heard the sound of the blade falling. He hadn't. He was still talking to someone on the phone. At least now, she would impede his ability to go further, to take her so far out into the bay she would never be found. This boat was not going anywhere after she'd cut the ignition wires.

She began to assess what other weapons were at her disposal. Gina had placed the purple scarf around her neck before she left the van. She was giving it back to Beth in hopes that it would be useful; also, they wanted to confuse the men about which woman was in the van and which woman wasn't. Attached to the scarf was a brooch with a sharp pin. That would make a nice weapon. She'd watched the man as he paced and noticed that he had a Ruger in a holster partly hidden by his shirt. That would put her at a disadvantage if he decided she was a threat. The way to negotiate these circumstances was to make him feel relaxed and at ease. Eventually, he put the phone down and opened another beer.

"Hey," she said, in a sultry a voice as she could manage. "I need to pee." He walked toward her and looked down.

"You do?" he said smiling at her. "Well now. We can't have you pissing on yourself." He chuckled. He reached for her and pulled her out of the cabin by her feet, which were bound with rope. "That means I'll have to untie your legs and pull down your pants for you." He grinned.

"I can't help that," she said. "You don't want me to make a mess do you?" Her hands were still tied, so he untied her feet and unbuttoned her jeans, pulling them down. He sat her on a can he had in the storage area and waited while she finished her business. When she finished, he licked his lips and unzipped his pants and pulled out his cock. He rubbed it back and forth in front of her. She felt like she was ready to puke on him, but if he thought she was repulsed, she would never get an opportunity. She waited patiently while he tried to spread her legs. He pulled her down and readied himself to take her. She did not hesitate. With all the strength she could muster from the muscles in the lower half of her body, she thrust her legs up and into his privates. He screamed in agony, bowled over into a ball.

She pulled up her pants, scooted back and snatched the brooch from the scarf. When he came at her in a rage, she tried to appear terrified. But as soon as he got close, she used the brooch to tear at his throat. He grabbed his throat and writhed on the floor of the boat. She reached for his gun and unsnapped the holster. She grabbed the gun and as he grabbed for it, he lost his balance. He listed like a beached whale on the side of the boat. She heard a plop and splash. But the light was so poor; she couldn't make out what had happened to him. She began to work on the bonds around her hands. She found a fishing knife inside a bucket in the storage area and cut the remaining threads.

She breathed heavily, trying to think what her next move should be. Before she could work out her next move, the man was back in the cabin and trying to choke her. She was about to black out when he slackened his grip. Maybe he thought there would be some reason to keep her alive; a ransom usually meant the person taken should be alive when returned. He slapped her. She saw stars, but struggled to recover her sight. Remember the fish bucket, she reached behind her and grabbed it, swinging it at his head. He was out.

This time, she didn't hesitate to remove herself from the boat, but how to do it. She was afraid to get in to water. All of her fears – about swimming, about drowning, about her parents' death – came rushing to assault her, worse than anything that idiot could do to her. She looked back at him. He was still out cold. She pocketed his cell phone and tied him up using the same rope he used to tie her. Then she lifted the kayak up and over the side of the boat. Her body trembled with the adrenaline rush. It landed with a splash in the water.

She heard voices from the shore, in the distance, the sound of a motor. Was it the other abductor or was it someone coming to help her? There was no time to decide. She lowered herself into the water and swam the few feet to the kayak. She tried three times to get into the kayak, but each time, she was unable to pull herself into it. Then, the thing flipped over, preventing her from getting in. Finally, she decided to rest for a while before trying again. She reached under the kayak and grabbed a handle to right it. This time, she pulled her body up and over the middle of the kayak, lying over the side. She bent her legs and pulled them over into the kayak. The oar was attached on the side. She pulled it out and into her hands. She took a moment to catch her breath and then tried to orient herself. Which way was south, north? She saw lights on the south side of the bay. She heard male voices. One of them sounded faintly like Ramon. A motor droned. She paddled toward the sounds.

Beth shivered with anxiety and with the need to warm herself. But when she could make out the form of Ramon in the small fishing boat her uncle used, she knew. She loved Ramon, irrevocably, without reservations, with all her heart. Alejandro held a flashlight and shone it in her eyes. She held up her hand to block out the light.

"Beth!" Ramon shouted. Alejandro maneuvered the little skiff toward the kayak, and Ramon reached for her. He pulled her into the little boat. "Are you all right?" he asked checking her over. He kissed her forehead and all over her face. She could hear the desperation in his voice.

"I thought I'd lost you, Beth," he said. "I'm never letting you out of my sight again." She was too exhausted to say more. Later, she explained that one of the abductors was in the boat and that it was disabled. They considered going back to get him, but noticed that the Coast Guard was already on its way. When they arrived at the pier near Gina's home, a crowd had gathered. Agency personnel were there. Ramon carried her into the house and helped her get changed and hydrated. "Do you need some time before you talk to them?" he asked looking into her eyes.

"No, time is important, I think," she said. She related the story to them of how she and Gina had been abducted. She told what she thought the kidnappers were after and then told how they had stolen a travel drive from her to give to someone named Arnold.

A local detective and an agent, Daxton Gow, from her former office stood there taking notes. She told them everything she could remember, and the detective then took off to give instructions to officers. Gow explained after the detective left that the property Arnold Dickens had stolen was not what he thought it was and that it would eventually find its way back to the agency. When he told Beth that he worked with Zah, her head snapped up and she looked at him inquiringly. He sat down beside her and looked her in the eyes.

"Yes," he said in low voice. "Both Ramon and Zah have helped to get you some backup here, so that there will be no problems. You needn't worry whether the information you were seeking will fall into Dickens' hands. It's been taken care of."

"What was it he wanted?" she asked.

"He was recruited by, well, I won't say who, but he was recruited to get a list of agent names and the strategic locations where they were last working," he said. "He thinks he's getting that, but instead, he's letting us know exactly where he is."

"Will they catch him so I don't have to worry about attempts on my life?" she asked. He looked at his watch and tapped it.

"As a matter of fact," he paused looking at the device. "He should be apprehended right. About. Now." He tapped the watch again and smiled at her.

"It's finished," he said. The two men who took you have both been taken into custody, and Dickens is headed for a federal prison cell." Beth visibly relaxed and buried her face in her hands.

"Hey, what are you doing to my fiancée?" Ramon said. He was standing near the kitchen bar to allow her to speak to the law enforcement officials. But now he approached them.

"Fiancée?" Beth said looking up at Ramon. He smiled sheepishly. "If that's a proposal, you're going to have to do better than that." She smiled back. Gow stood up and said his goodbyes. Ramon shook his hand and closed the doors. He sat down on the couch with her.

"Sorry, sweetheart," he said. "I meant to make this a more romantic proposal, but I just couldn't wait. I never want to let you out of my sight again. I nearly died when I realized those freaks had abducted you. I should have been watching you better. Can you forgive me?"

"There's nothing to forgive," she said, placing a hand on his cheek. "I'm exhausted, Ramon; let's have a rest and we can talk more later." They retired to the room Gina had given Beth. The large bed suited them both. Beth watched as Ramon took off his shirt, his gun and pants. She had taken a shower and lay in the bed waiting for him to join her. She felt the bed dip as he placed a knee on the side and slid under the covers beside her. He put his arms around her. She laid her head on his chest and heard the thumping of his heart and the sound of his breathing. They lay like that for some time before he spoke. He rubbed her arm and turned to look at her.

"I understand if you don't want to," he said. "Did they?"

"No," she said, taking a deep breath. "Cullen tried, but had his family jewels kicked into the next century."

"Ouch," he said. "The asshole deserved it." He kissed her on the head and nuzzled her on the neck. She felt an answering wetness and a stirring in her abdomen. There was no mistaking her need for him. "I can't wait, Beth." He looked at her as if asking permission to begin. She nodded and put her arms around him as he positioned himself at her core and pushed slowly inside her. He rested there for a while before he began to pump vigorously. When they both shattered with their climax, they sank into a mind numbing, peaceful sleep. Just before they drifted off, Ramon heard her say, "I love you, Ramon."

The next day, everyone woke late, and Aunt Maddy made brunch. Uncle Gerald took Alejandro on a tour of his laboratory. They went to the pier where they had docked Gerald's little boat and secured the kayak. Mateo drove into town on an errand for Ramon and returned just as everyone was preparing to take a short walk to the end of the street where people who enjoyed fishing and birding tended to gather. When Gina, Aunt Maddy, Uncle Gerald, Mateo and Alejandro were gathered in the sitting area, Ramon brought flowers to Beth as she sat on the couch, looking at family pictures. Ramon had given everyone but Beth a clue as to what would happen next. Knowing that Brazilian jazz was Beth's favorite music, Ramon put some on through a speaker that Gina had in her sitting area. When Beth realized the tension in the room had changed, she looked up to see what was going on. A bunch of red roses was thrust at her, and she laughed and moved back. Ramon was behind the large bouquet. He grinned at her.

He handed them to her. She looked at him and then at the faces of her family. They were all smiling at her. "What's this about?" she asked, standing up. Ramon got on one knee and took her hand in his. They turned off the music and clapped softly, laughing and grinning as Ramon cleared his throat and looked nervous. She could see a fine mist of perspiration on his brow. He wiped his forehead and took a deep breath.

"Ms. Ethel Elizabeth Larsen," he paused and took a small box from his pants pocket and opened it. "Would you do me the honor of becoming my wife?" She looked down at his hand holding hers and at the large diamond ring in the box. Gina and Aunt Maddy gasped and held each other as they waited for her answer. She looked over at her sister and aunt, and they nodded encouragingly at her. Aunt Maddy motioned as though she was taking too long. She looked at the faces of his brothers Alejandro and Mateo, who were both grinning. She felt him shift on his knee.

Doubts rushed at her. Was this the right thing to do? Would his family accept her? Would she be happy with a man so much younger than her? Would he be happy with her? Would he grow tired of her someday when she was much older? But, if she didn't take this chance, she might not ever get another. She wasn't getting any younger, and time had already evaporated for her. It was time for her to reach for her own dreams and to let the rest of it work itself out.

"Beth?" he looked up at her.

"Yes, Ramon," she said, letting out a breath. "Yes, I will marry you." He stood up and embraced her, lifting her off her feet and twirling her around in a circle. He grinned and kissed her. "You have made me so happy," he said. "I promise to make you happy."

15 ONE IS MISSING

Gow drove to the sheriff's office where they detained the criminals responsible for trying to steal highly sensitive government information. He had checked the hospital earlier to see whether he could get any information from the man who was clocked by the old lady. But the thug only remembered being hired by someone named Arnold. After showing his government credentials, Gow walked into the office where detectives and officers had their desks.

He was handed a clipboard with information on it regarding the men in custody. "Shit!" he said, dropping the clipboard. Deputy Cooper paused, frowning at him. "We caught Logan with the travel drive, not Dickens," he said. Logan had taken the drive, borrowed a friend's computer and plugged it in.

"What's the problem? We have them ready to be interrogated," Cooper said.

"One is missing," Gow said. "We still have a bad actor on the loose. I need to find out where he is." After a long session of interrogation with Logan and Cullen, Gow texted Ramon.

Gow: Heads up, Ramon, we're looking for Arnold

Dickens; we think he's a contractor.

He heard nothing back. So he decided to get a location from Zah. However, she wasn't available and not online. He ran a hand through his hair and figured it might be good to track down Ramon.

Ramon used a key to open the door to the house on Avenue P1/2. It was eerily quiet in the house. The hair on the back of his neck bristled. He felt someone had been here. Ramon and Beth both pulled their weapons. But he checked all the rooms and found nothing. Neither did Beth, who also had the same sense that something was not right and helped check everything.

"The alarms did not go off," he said. "So everything looks all right." They put their guns away. He gathered her in his arms and hugged her and then walked her over to the couch where they sat down. "I'm the luckiest man in the world," he said nuzzling her.

"I'm pretty lucky too," she said, smiling. "I need to tell you something important," she said, remembering her vow to tell him how she felt when she was trapped on the boat. "I love you." He looked at her, bending down to look into her eyes.

"Oh, Beth," he said. "I'm so happy to hear you say that. Of course, I knew all along that you loved me," he said, laughing. She playfully hit him on the arm.

"So you did," she said. "You're pretty sure of yourself."

"Only sure of how much I love you too, Beth," he said, kissing her deeply. Then, he withdrew and smoothed a hand over her hair, pulling her into his lap on the couch.

"But what about the rest of your family?" she asked after some time.

"They will be fine with it," he said. "You'll see. We have so many people in this family, you'll need a contacts list to keep up with all of them."

"But what about your mother?" she asked.

"My mother wants me to be happy. And," he placed a finger lightly on her nose, "you, my pretty lady, make me happy." He grinned. She turned from him and sat down beside him on the couch.

"It's been a hard time," she said. "I think I need some rest, Ramon."

"I'll get us some wine and run a hot bath for you, sweetheart. Mateo is going to drive your car over here from the business district," he said. She had given her car keys to Ramon that morning, almost too exhausted to worry about the Honda. She walked upstairs and to the bedroom they shared. She began to take off her shirt and froze as she heard a distinct thump.

Ramon frowned as he looked out the kitchen window. He noticed something was not quite right about the window. It was cracked, as though someone had carelessly left it open. He closed and locked it. Alejandro and Mateo had returned to Houston. The friends they had watching the area were likely gone now too. The alarm had been canceled. All was supposedly good. But something told Ramon that things were not right. He had an unsettling feeling.

He looked at the kitchen window and out the back from the pool area. Nothing seemed amiss. So he poured a glass of wine for both Beth and for himself. He checked the house one more time, making certain the windows were locked and the doors secured. He checked the small alcove at the back of the house and was headed back toward the living room when a heavy object hit him in the head and everything went black.

Beth walked back downstairs with her weapon drawn and pointed, checking each room. She saw broken glass and wine on the floor. She shivered, no Ramon. The boards of the floor creaked as she walked to the back of the house. Just then, an arm reached for her gun and a fist rammed into her jaw, cutting her cheek. She was stunned, but not completely insensate. A heavy arm drew her up; she felt herself being carried out the back door and to a little house in the back.

She threw up, as her head hung down the back of the man carrying her. Then, she lost a sense of time again. She felt herself being thrown on a mattress and her blouse being removed. Time seemed to be floating just out of her reach. She couldn't tell whether it was day or night or whether she was up or down. She felt a wave of fear and nausea come over her again. But a cup of water was thrust to her lips and she drank thirstily.

"Wake up, bitch," a gruff voice said. Everything was blurry and came slowly into focus. A splash of water hit her face; she finally focused on the figure before her. She struggled to place the face; then realized it was the man from the New York bar. How could that be? She shook her head. A mistake. Her jaw throbbed. But suddenly she became very alert as the man tied her wrists and pinned her to the bed. He stood before her with his cock jutting out. He grinned, stroking his penis.

"I've been waiting to get you, you little cunt," he said, licking his lips. "Just looking at you makes me cum." He pulled her jeans off and then ripped off her underwear but had not tied her legs. She used her legs as weapons and kept fighting him, but he struck her again. She stopped struggling for a moment to regain her senses. Maybe she could buy some time if she could talk him out of rape. He bent down and kissed her and pinched her breasts, twisting her nipple. She fought the urge to black out again. His cock rubbed against her stomach. He pulled back to hover over her.

"What's your name?" she asked.

"What do you need to know my name for, bitch? I just want to fuck you. Open your legs."

Gina sat up in her bed, gasping. Something was wrong with Beth. She could feel it. She dressed quickly and drove to Ramon's house. Something made her go to the back of the house. She was drawn to a house across the alley. She heard noises, the sounds of struggling, grunting, a male voice, cursing. She walked up the steps in the house and rounded a corner and walked to the head of the bed where her sister was spread eagle, a man standing over her. She looked at the man and smiled, pointed her finger at him and moved it from side to side, suggesting that he was doing wrong. Then, she turned and walked swiftly out the door.

Arnold thought he was seeing double at first. Then, he realized this must be the twin Logan and Cullen had spoken of. He looked down at the woman tied to the headboard and realized in his frenzied greed that he could have two women for the trouble of one. He took off to search for the other woman; he looked in all the rooms in the house, which was not large, but had hidden places. Finally, he returned to his prey.

When Ramon came to, his head was throbbing, but he knew that time was important. Gina found him and helped him get untied. She explained what she'd seen and shaking with fear, urged him to hurry. Arnold Dickens was following her, but he might go back to Beth. His hands trembling, he found the locked cabinet with weapons, used the combination to open the lock and took out a Smith and Wesson XVR 460. He loaded it and moved to the back of the house. He saw small drops of blood leading to a house on the other side of the alley. His suspicion was confirmed when he saw vomit. He must have hit her hard. He cocked the gun.

Arnold had waited a long time to take this woman; he decided not to waste time chasing her sister and returned to Beth. When he got to the bed, she had loosed one hand and was struggling to get the other untied. His cock was so hard he could hardly stand it. When he got her in the house the first time, he came when he got her top off. It didn't take long for him to be ready for her. He knelt on the bed between her legs, trying to hold them down as she struggled. He nearly came again as he tried to prepare to lie on top of her. But suddenly, a hard object hit him in the head, knocking him to the floor so forcefully that he rolled to the window. Vela, the bastard. How did he get in here? The sister. He grabbed for the gun on the table before him, but before he could cock it, a bullet lodged in his chest. He fell to the floor. Ramon checked the man. No pulse.

Ramon rushed to Beth and untied her wrists; he held her in his arms. She shook with terror and shock. "It's OK, sweetheart," he said, rocking her. "He'll never hurt you again." He helped her get dressed and handed Gina his phone. Gina called Gow, letting him know what had happened. When Gow and his partner arrived, they took in the scene, got a brief statement from Beth and her sister and let the couple go back to their home. "We'll take care of everything from here," he told Ramon. "Just go take care of your woman," he said, looking at an ashen Beth. "I think she needs a little time to recover. Two incidents in as many days — that is quite a bit for anyone to cope with. We'll wait to talk to her again later."

Ramon carried her back to the house and sat her on the bed.

"Do you want to go to the hospital, Beth?" he asked. "Did he?"

She shook her head no. "No, he didn't have a chance. I just want to be left alone. I don't want to be poked and prodded or asked questions. I just want some peace. To be left alone for a while." Gina appeared in the door of the bedroom and walked over to her. She hugged her sister. "Are you going to be OK?" Gina asked. Beth nodded. "Why was that psycho after you, Beth?"

Beth's hands shook as she smoothed hair from her face. "I'll explain it all later, Gina," she said. "Right now, I need some rest." Gina nodded and agreed that she needed some rest too. She gave her sister another hug and went home.

Later, Ramon ran water for a bath and put her in the tub. After bathing her, he put her under the covers and gave her a warm cup of red wine. He held her close.

She shuddered, sighed and sank into the covers, wrapped in Ramon's arms.

EPILOGUE

Beth and Ramon enjoyed a raucous engagement party at the Vela family restaurant in Houston. A band was hired that played an assortment of Latin and American tunes. Tables were laden with food of all kinds. Beth and Ramon made a few of their signature dishes, shrimp quesadillas, salmon wraps and potato frittata. Gina and Aunt Maddy made Hazelnut Buttercacke and truffle deviled eggs along with Seattle tuna rolls. Ramon's mother and the restaurant cook made black bean rice, chicken mushroom quesadillas, shrimp tacos, and enchiladas. The tables included eggplant fritters, sausage rolls, crab balls and an assortment of other food. Wine, beer and wine coolers kept the party lively.

When Beth met Ramon's mother, well before the party, they came to a meeting of the minds. "I try not to interfere in the lives of my children, Beth," she said. "I know that you are quite a bit older than Ramon, but he is the baby and he has always been indulged." She said that last part as though Beth should understand that she was being embraced because Ramon's mother loved her son and her other children.

During the engagement party there was a long period

of meeting Ramon's other relatives and friends. Gina dressed in a bright pink dress, which attracted the attention of more than one single man at the party, including an increasingly possessive Mateo – much to Gina's surprise. Aunt Maddy and Uncle Gerald danced at least once before Aunt Maddy had to take a rest. Aunt Maddy and Ramon's mother had a long chat while the young people enjoyed their salsa dancing. Alejandro, Isabella, Rosa, Mateo and Nicolito were there with their spouses and friends. Ramon's father, Nicolas, a tall handsome man with dark greying hair, laughed heartily while talking to Uncle Gerald.

Beth met Barbara. "I heard that he was going to marry you," Barbara said, sounding defensive. The band played "La Vida es un Carnaval" as they talked. "I don't think he should have asked someone his own age, but I can't do anything about that," she said.

"But I think you mistake things," Beth said. Barbara looked at her, astonished. Beth whispered to Barbara.

"You mean, you. … " Barbara stuttered. "You're. … Girl, you have been taking good care of yourself. You look half your age." Beth nodded her head, smiling. They both laughed. Barbara laughed so hard that tears formed at the corners of her eyes. She took another sip of her margarita, and said, "Honey, if you need anything, anything at all, you call on Barbara." She strutted off to dance with a man of indeterminate age who appeared too shy to ask women to dance.

Beth tried taking a sip of wine, but her stomach had been upset all week. She wondered whether she needed to see her doctor. Hopefully, it was nothing serious. Familiar arms grabbed her from behind. Ramon nuzzled her and whispered in her ear. "Hey!" she said, grinning. They could hear the band playing "Suavemente" in the distance. He laughed and rubbed his erection against her plump behind. He pulled her into one of the back rooms and massaged her breasts. He pulled up her plum-colored skirt and lifted her legs around his waist. He fingered her wet slit and found that she was more than ready. When he entered her, he pulled his head back and looked into her eyes. "You are the most delicious woman I have ever had the pleasure of loving . . ." He shut his eyes and pulled back and surged into her again, and again until they both collapsed.

"This is the way to celebrate an engagement," he said, cradling her head against his chest as they sat in a nearby chair.

"Oh, Ramon," she said. "Did I hear you say something about loving me?" she asked in a sultry voice.

"I did. I do," he waited, hoping to hear her say the words. She bit his ear lobe gently. "I love you too," she said, smiling.

"I know," he grinned.

A week later, they were married on the beach in Galveston, with a Mariachi band in attendance and a score of friends and family to witness their commitment to one another. Her sister was her matron of honor. They settled on staying at Ramon's house on Avenue P1/2 for the time being. A few weeks after the wedding, Beth was looking through her email in the safe room and discovered an email from Zah.

Zah: Found your mysterious missing couple.

Beth hesitated before responding. She was surprised to hear from Zah.

Beth: Can you say where they are?

Zah: They've been working under deep cover. I wouldn't be surprised if their daughter gets a call from them soon.

Beth smiled.

Beth: Thanks, Zah.

Zah: No problem, Beth. Have a happy life.

Two weeks later, Beth visited her doctor and sat on the examining table waiting for news. Ramon walked in, after having stepped out to give Beth some privacy while she was being examined. He was reluctant to stay for that portion of the visit. When the doctor walked in in her white jacket and dark pants, she looked at them both and said, "Mr. Vela, could you please sit down?" He frowned at her and sat down gingerly in the chair.

"Congratulations," she said. "You're going to be parents." They both looked at each other, stunned at the realization that their lives would change.

"But I thought. ..." Beth said, her voice trailing off.

"That it was too late," the doctor said smiling. "Many women do. Let's get you ready for the big event, shall we?"

Seven months later, Ramon and Beth welcomed healthy twins into their lives.

Long before the couple settled into a life of changing diapers and taking turns walking colicky babies, Beth contacted Val to tell her of her discovery about her parents. The McKeans had been undercover for some time. They had been captured but rescued in a covert mission. Some of the individuals in the group they had been assigned to help did not make it back safely, but the names and the sensitive information about their whereabouts was kept secret. Some of those individuals were still working undercover in sensitive roles that needed protection. Later, a woman drove up to a house in New Jersey. She knocked on the door and removed her large, dark sunglasses. Val McKean Standridge felt her knees buckle and her vision go black. Her husband, Brice, caught her and held her to him. "Can I help you?" he asked.

"I'm Val's mother, Helen," she said, smiling. Having seen plenty of photographs of his mother-in-law, he opened the door to let her in; she sat in the spacious living room waiting for her daughter to recover. When Val came to, she reached out to touch her mother who was sitting beside her. "Are you real?" Val asked.

"I'm real, Valerie," Val's mother said, hugging her daughter to her. Two days later, Val's father, Benjamin, joined the family, and they enjoyed a heartfelt reunion, complete with grandchildren and lots of catching up. The McKeans were now officially retired, but still keeping a low profile. When Val heard why her parents had been missing for so long, it took a while for her to forgive them, but eventually, she did.

Engaging Passion is a work of fiction. Names, characters, places and incidents are products of the writer's imagination or have been used fictitiously and are not to be construed as real. Any resemblance to persons living or dead, actual events, places, incidents or organizations is coincidental.

Cover design by Tatiana Villa

The Hot Desire Series:

Heat -

Hot -

Desire at Sea –

Engaging Passion –

Blog with Ela Bell at Narrativemagic.com.
http://www.narrative-magic.squarespace.com/ela-bell/

Review *Heat, Hot, Desire at Sea, and Engaging Passion* at any ebook outlet.

Would you like to receive a newsletter from Narrativemagic.com about Ela Bell's upcoming novels? Write at narrativemagic@gmail.com

ABOUT THE AUTHOR

Ela Bell has written fiction for a number of years and is a member of RWA. She has a degree in literature and writes the occasional poem. Bell publishes under the pen names Kate Ayre Campbell and Ela Bell and has written three other novellas in the Hot Desire series—*Heat, Hot,* and *Desire at Sea.* She welcomes email from her readers. Write to her at elabell19@gmail.com.